MIKE LANTRY

---◆---

A GUNMAN
CLOSE BEHIND

Complete and Unabridged

LINFORD
Leicester

Originally published in Great Britain in 1957

First Linford Edition
published 2005

Copyright © 1957 by Anthony A. Glynn

British Library CIP Data

Lantry, Mike
    A gunman close behind.—Large print ed.—
Linford mystery library
    1. Detective and mystery stories
    2. Large type books
    I. Title
    823.9'14 [F]

    ISBN 1–84395–788–4

Published by
F. A. Thorpe (Publishing)
Anstey, Leicestershire

Set by Words & Graphics Ltd.
Anstey, Leicestershire
Printed and bound in Great Britain by
T. J. International Ltd., Padstow, Cornwall

This book is printed on acid-free paper

A GUNMAN CLOSE BEHIND

Mike Lantry, the tough, hard-bitten chief of World Wide Investigations, was on his way back to New York after a restful vacation when he gave a ride to a lone girl on an Indiana highway. Lantry was up to his neck in it from that moment on, coming into contact with gun-wielding hoodlums and crooked cops. When he joins forces with plucky Joanne Kilvert to pull down a crook's empire, he embarks on a tense chase in which, for every inch of the action-packed way, there is a gunman close behind.

1

Ever hear that old saying about massive oaks starting out as tiny acorns?

There's a lot in it. I know.

I once brought a big ruckus down on my head simply because I gave a girl a ride during a rainstorm.

I was bringing back a neat line in sun-tan from Florida. Three weeks of lying on the beaches were at my back; I had been away from it all while another hand steered World Wide Investigations from its headquarters on Madison Avenue, New York City.

Now I was heading back in a roundabout way, driving through Indiana to pay a surprise call on an old buddy, Jack Kay, up in South Bend.

I remember the way I felt. Glowing and newly charged with energy. The coupe hummed along the highway as though in tune to the brassy swing number blaring out of the car radio.

The world seemed all right.

The southland, with the motels where I spent the last couple of nights, was behind me, as were the Indiana towns of Indianapolis, Westfield, Kokomo and Peru.

The sudden summer shower started somewhere between Peru and Plymouth. There was a white flimmer of lightning off on the flat horizon. A cluster of black clouds boiled up over the highway and big drops of rain came slashing down in a deluge. I wound up the hood of the coupe quickly.

It was growing dark fast.

Twenty minutes of driving through the downpour, and I saw the girl.

She was walking towards Plymouth, humping a grip, a slight figure out on the rain-slicked highway. As I drew nearer, I could see she wore only a light summer costume, clinging to her, as sodden as if she had been capering fully clothed in the nearby swamps.

I hit the brakes a little way past her and called back through the rain:

'Want a ride?'

2

She came forward cautiously, and I saw her face, heart-shaped, elfin and with strands of short-cut black hair rain-plastered around it. She was somewhere around twenty-four.

I sat with the door of the coupe held open, turned about to face her.

The engine thrummed and the big drops of rain hit the car like wet bullets.

Maybe it was the scar on my face, sometimes I catch sight of myself in a mirror and realise how like a bad guy in a 'B' movie it makes me appear. She came gingerly through the curtain of rain, as though I was a Grimm goblin. Then she hastened her pace and hefted the grip into the car.

'I'm going to South Bend,' I said. 'Where are you making for?'

'South Bend,' she answered. Her voice was breathless and held an odd mixture of fear and thankfulness.

In my racket you get to sizing up people by their speech and actions almost by instinct. There was something on this girl's mind for sure.

She settled herself into the seat beside

me, with the grip on the floor. Before I kicked the car forward, she turned her head for a long look at the gloomy, rain-swept highway behind. I could see the scared look on her face. It was as if she expected the devil himself to come whooping along from the direction of Peru.

I wondered what she was running from, but that was no concern of mine, I was just a guy giving her a ride to South Bend.

Sneaking a look at her in the imperfect light, I saw definite signs of strain on her pretty, rain-wet features. She looked like somebody's kid sister from anywhere at all; wet, shivery and, above all, scared.

We made the usual, meaningless small-talk about the weather as the headlights picked out a path on the glistening highway.

At one point the sound of a vehicle came purring upon us from the rear. The girl turned hastily, half ducked behind the back of the seat and looked out of the rear window. I saw fear written clear across her face as she watched the rain-distorted lights gain on us.

It was merely a bus heading for Plymouth. As she turned about again, the girl threw me a self-conscious glance which I saw but pretended not to notice. The fear, almost terror, in her face had me worried.

The bus rocketed by, its lighted windows dwindling before us in the watery darkness. A little world of people passing in the night.

I thought it was a smart idea to get to know her name, in case I heard of a young woman missing from somewhere or other, so I said:

'My name's Mike Lantry, by the way.' I tried to make it casual.

She looked at me quickly and said: 'The Investigator?' There was a tone to her voice that gave me a premonition of something other than the driving rain being in the wind.

I nodded.

'I'm Joanne Kilvert,' she said.

Right then, just as I was about to take a sudden bend in the road, she turned to look out of the rear window. I heard her give a little squeak and saw her duck down in the seat.

'It's them,' she said urgently and huskily. 'Put your foot down — they mustn't see me!'

I could see her face, white and terror-stricken, in the glow of the dashboard. She was as scared as a kitten, and it was catching.

Automatically, without any questions, I gave the car the gun as we approached the bend. I took a quick glance over my shoulder to see a big sedan whirring along about a hundred and fifty yards behind, slashing the curtain of rain with powerful headlamps.

We took the bend almost on two wheels. The headlights picked out a stand of trees to our left, splitting their dark bulk was a dirt road. Without hesitation, I put the coupe into a screeching turn and headed up the dirt road. The big sedan had yet to make the turn in the highway, but it would be in sight any second.

Going up that dirt road may have been a fool thing to do, but it was the most immediate way of avoiding that sedan, and the stark terror on Joanne Kilvert's face prompted me to make use of this one chance of keeping whoever followed us from seeing her.

I stopped over a hump in the dirt road and switched off the engine and lights. We were deep in the trees. We sat waiting, panting as though we had just run clear from Peru.

Through the trees we saw the sedan come into view. It went flashing past, a black streak on the highway, the white spears of its headlights slithering off the rain-polished boles of the trees.

Then it was gone.

'Who's in that car?' I asked.

'Some men I want to avoid.'

I boiled over at that.

'That's as obvious as hell,' I told her, 'or have you taken it on the lam from some happy hatch?'

She made no reply but grabbed my arm.

'They're coming back!' She breathed the words urgently, and I could just see her wide eyes in the darkness.

Back from the direction in which it had

originally travelled rocketed the black sedan. The headlamps flashed almost angrily through the interstices of the trees down by the highway. It came to a sudden stop close to the opening of the dirt road, its brakes keening on a high note.

'They'll come up here!' Joanne Kilvert's voice was a panic-edged whisper.

'No they won't,' I told her. 'Get out and stay put.'

I flung the door of the coupe open and almost pushed her out of the car. A sharp needle of impatience jabbed at me as she began to lug the grip after her.

'Don't bother with that.'

'I must — they mustn't get it.'

When she was clear of the car, I slammed the engine into life, whirled the vehicle about in the narrow confines of the tree-fringed dirt road and went jouncing down towards the highway. In making the turn, my headlights picked out a picture of the girl standing up against a tree. She looked lost and frightened, and I suddenly felt desperately sorry for her.

Down at the highway, three men had

issued from the sedan and were in the act of entering the dark corridor of the dirt road.

They were all of medium size and had a sameness about them, like cops — or crooks. In my headlights I saw they all wore black overcoats and fedoras.

I braked.

'Lookin' for someone?' I called over the mingled purring of my motor and that of the sedan parked on the far side of the wet-glossed highway. I tried to make my voice sound like that of an Indiana hick.

One of the trio walked towards my coupe. Under the brim of the snappy fedora, I saw a lean, high-cheekboned face with a carefully clipped moustache curving under an Italian nose. His eyes were dark and had an odd flatness. The high contours of his face glistened wetly.

He stood close to the rolled-down window of the coupe, looking at me. The engines purred and the rain spattered on the leaves high above our heads.

'You had a girl in your car,' he said. I didn't know whether it was a statement or a question. His two friends stood around

9

in the background with their hands deep in their coat pockets, looking like characters in a *circa* 1930 gangster movie.

'Yeah, sure. My girl Beaulah,' I replied in my hick voice, jerking my thumb over my shoulder at the dirt road. I had a notion these characters weren't fooled by the hick accent; it didn't go well with my lightweight sharkskin suit, my car or my general appearance. But I persevered. 'She lives at a farm back up the road a piece. We just been to a movie in Peru — '

'We thought,' said the man with the moustache, cutting me off in the middle of my hick act, 'that you might have picked up a girl who was walking along the highway — a girl with a grip.'

'No, we didn't pick anybody up.'

'You put on some speed when we came behind you.'

'Yep, I guess I did at that. I had to put my foot down some what with it gettin' late an' my girl's folks bein' so strict on her. You fellas cops? Is somethin' wrong?'

'Not cops. We just wondered if you saw the girl.'

The guy with the clipped moustache

spoke coldly and watched me with those flat eyes. I still had a feeling he wasn't fooled by my hick talk. I remembered passing a smaller road branching off the highway shortly before I met up with the girl, and I recalled the name painted on a signboard close to it.

'She could've gotten a ride on a car or truck that turned off on the Logansport road, or maybe took the bus into Plymouth,' I offered.

'Maybe she did at that.'

As though that was the curtain-line at the close of some play, they turned on their heels and walked towards the sedan. I sat there in the purring coupe, watched the sedan start up and move off around the bend in the direction of Peru. Maybe they were going to scout along that Logansport road.

That, it seemed, was that; so I climbed out and hoofed it up the dirt road, leaving the motor of the coupe running.

Joanne Kilvert was still standing against the tree. The darkness and the rain made her only half-distinguishable, but I could see she held the grip, clinging to it as if it was her rich uncle.

I'm a hard man, the life I've led has made me so. Kicking around with a gun in one pocket and a dollar to keep you from the poor-house in the other, the way I was before the agency got to be a big thing, and Mike Lantry was just another shamus with a shiny pants' seat, is a good way to acquire a hard shell. But there are chinks in the armour. I still have feelings, and I felt sorry as hell for the lost kid standing against that tree.

I began to regret that crack about her being an escapee from a happy hatch; though, for all I knew, she could have been.

'They've gone,' I said. 'I'm sorry I lost my temper there a couple of minutes ago.'

'Have they really gone? Are you sure?'

My grudging apology seemed to go unheeded. The fear of the men in the sedan was uppermost in her mind.

'Sure. Let's get back to the car.'

The rain slackened as we walked down the dirt road to the highway. Joanne Kilvert kept close to me as we approached the wet banner of asphalt. Belatedly, I took the grip from her to hump it down to the coupe.

We made no conversation as I kicked the car into action and swung out of the side-road, turning for Plymouth.

The snort of an engine sounded behind us, and the sedan reappeared, humming around the bend again like a beast lunging out of ambush.

Joanne Kilvert turned about in her seat, terror mirrored on her face, and her mouth quivering.

'They're coming after us,' she gasped. 'They didn't go away, they only went around the bend and waited for a glimpse of me. They saw me get into the car.' She seemed almost paralysed with fear. Whoever the guys in the black coats and fedoras were, they had the dark-haired girl about as scared as any human being I had seen — and frightened people were no novelty to me.

I hit the accelerator hard enough to come within a fraction of slamming the pedal through the floor. The car zoomed up the wet highway, running from the sedan like an alley-cat beating it from the toughest dog in the neighbourhood. The premonition I felt a short time before came back and rankled. I was getting mixed up in something. I didn't know what it was, and I was growing sore as hell.

'Who are they?' I asked the girl.

She didn't answer, she was still twisted about in the seat, watching the big sedan chasing us maybe a hundred yards behind. I grew real mean and snarled. 'Look, I'm nobody's fall guy. When I'm chased, I like to know who's after me. Maybe that's kind of old-fashioned to you, but that's the way I was brought up. Are those guys cops or hoods? Sometimes the resemblance between the two species is so close you can't tell one from the other.'

The sedan was gaining on us. I gave the coupe the gun again and felt I was the biggest patsy of all time. I could hold my own in the concrete jungle of New York, but someone was making a chump of me out in the Indiana sticks. The girl still did not answer.

Mean is not the word for how I felt right then.

14

'Who the hell are those guys?' I demanded in the tones they use in the back rooms of police stations when they have a firm grip on the rubber persuaders.

The sedan growled after us, swallowing up the miles.

'They're Athelstan Shelmerdine's men,' she replied in a voice little more than a whisper.

That rocked me from the roots of my hair to the cuticles of my toenails. I crouched over the wheel like an eager jockey and watched the blurred, headlamp-whitened highway ribboning out of the blackness and flashing under the car.

Athelstan Shelmerdine! Hell!

Shelmerdine, the big-time racketeer who had his fingers in every illegal enterprise within who-knew-how-big a radius of Chicago. Shelmerdine, who sat behind a façade of respectable businesses and pulled strings that made all sorts of things happen on various levels of the under-world and upperworld. Shelmerdine, who graduated from being a booze-runner in the prohibition days to the new style in gang-moguls. Shelmerdine, who owned people outright; who waxed fat on super thievery and on whom nobody could pin anything.

And a bunch of his mugs were tailing us.

And my Browning was packed away in my grip which, in turn, was locked away in the boot.

I said nothing for a long time, I just concentrated on putting distance between the sedan and my own car. But the black overcoats and fedora hats were no slouches when it came to getting life out of a car. The sedan stuck to us too close for comfort.

'How the blazes did *you* fall foul of Shelmerdine?' I asked Joanne Kilvert.

She was crouching low in her seat, tensed and frightened.

'It's a long story,' she said. She never took her wide eyes from the driving mirror, in which the pursuing sedan was reflected, as she spoke. 'It's a long story, but have you heard of Arthur Kilvert?'

I watched the highway racing up out of the night with one eye and with the other watched the gleaming headlights of the car behind us in the driving mirror.

I remembered the name Arthur Kilvert and went riffling through a mental card-index for the connection. Over the years I've developed a faculty for stowing away data inside my skull. It becomes almost second nature after a while, like the photographic eye some cops develop so they can spot a face or a way of walking or even the special way a guy lights a cigarette or flips back his hat, though a number of years have passed since they first noted the mannerism.

The Arthur Kilvert connection was not a matter of years away, only months. I jockeyed the coupe, watched that black beast of a sedan roaring along behind us, and the story came seeping to the surface.

'Yes, I remember,' I told the girl. 'Arthur Kilvert was an official in a trade union in Chicago. Seemed to be a right guy and resented the racketeers who began to shove their noses in, trying to pull the strings of his union as they did in so many others. Kilvert didn't care for the new style of protection racket and said so loud and clear and wrote so in black and white. He began crusading and got to be a regular bug in the hair with the racket-boys . . . '

I tailed off and got to thinking about the rest of the Arthur Kilvert story. It was ugly.

I only knew the case from newspaper reports, black words on pulp paper telling of a man who tried to play it square and what became of him. Telling of a car screeching to a stop close to the front lawn of a house in a Chicago suburb where a man, his wife and child romped in the warmth of a summer afternoon — Sunday afternoon.

Sunday afternoon shattered by the screech of brakes, rent by the hard stutter of a sub-machine gun with the snort and growl of a hastily started car as an anti-climax.

That had been the way of it. Arthur Kilvert paid off for being a straight citizen, paid off prohibition-day fashion. Only this was Chicago in the nineteen-fifties, not the 'twenties.

'You're Kilvert's widow?' I asked.

I was concentrating on keeping an even

distance between the coupe and Shelmerdine's hoods and, so far, I was doing fine. I was watching the highway, but I could see the girl's features reflected in the windshield. A hardness had taken possession of them now, the kind of hardness you see in a woman's face after all the tears have been cried away.

'No, not his wife, his sister. My sister-in-law survived the shooting, but she's worse off than Arthur. She walks on crutches now because she doesn't have a left leg any more, but they injured her mind worse than her body. She saw Arthur shot down before her eyes, and the baby was killed in her arms. She's twenty-four years old.'

Nothing about crookdom surprises or disgusts me any more, I know it from the soles of its stinking feet to the roots of its lousy hair. There was a time when a thing like the shooting at the Kilvert home would have made me spit — or maybe vomit. But I know the ways of the big-time thieves too well now. A man, his wife, his baby are as nothing to them in their climb towards dirty riches. Nothing at all, not even the ashes and dust the Book says they are.

There was no more time or opportunity for philosophy. Joanne Kilvert was turned about in her seat again, she suddenly clutched my arm in alarmed urgency.

'They're going to shoot!' she cried. 'Get down!'

The little world of the car was an enclosed box, thrumming to the pulse of the engine, rocking to the whirr of the wheels. Outside, the growl of the pursuing sedan was sounding loud. I saw the car in the mirror, pulling out into the centre of the highway, positioning itself with one of the overcoats and fedoras leaning from a window with something in his hand.

Joanne Kilvert crouched down to the floor, close to the grip that seemed so important to her. I pressed the accelerator down to the floor boards, and the outside world was a liquid blur of racing shadows.

The mobster with the gun seemed to wait a hell of a time before opening up. But he did eventually.

Three shots bellowed out, and I put the coupe into a zig-zag. One slug spanged into the bodywork of the car somewhere at the back, one ripped the fabric of the hood, and the third must have been a complete miss. Maybe the Shelmerdine hoods were just trying to scare us into stopping, maybe they were trying to hit our tyres.

I was cursing loudly because my Browning was packed up with my T-shirts in the boot.

'These mugs must want you awful bad,' I told Joanne Kilvert.

Then I doused all the lights and drove blind. I wondered, with a detached and cynical part of my mind, why a police highway patrol was never around when you needed one. Right now, a couple of motor-cycle cops would be useful, even if I was over-reaching the speed limit and driving without lights.

Another couple of shots sounded from behind, and the slugs went zipping past the coupe.

Then I saw the twist in the road, only just in time. Travelling at the rate the coupe was hitting and without lights, that bend came at me out of the blackness. I whirled the wheel to the right quickly, heard the huddled girl squeal as the car lurched and saw a big bill-board go flashing past the window on her side of the coupe. We must have been within inches of hitting that wooden bill-board.

I didn't wait to give my heart a chance to settle down after turning the bend, but kept my foot hard on the gas and burned up the highway.

Maybe the girl and I had been extra good during the immediate past; we must have done something, one or the other of us, to deserve the break we were given at that moment.

In the blackness at our backs, something ear-splitting happened. An edgy keening of brakes merged into a splintering crash. Then a silence more frightening than the noise.

Joanne Kilvert and I turned about to look out of the rear window.

'They crashed,' she whispered. 'They hit the bill-board on the turning.'

A vivid little cameo was dwindling away into the darkness behind us. The sedan piled up against the bill-board, a flicker of flames starting into life at its hood. Figures were scuttling out of the wrecked car. The headlamps were still on, and their light, combined with the erratic glow of the flames, showed the mocking face of the ten-times-larger-than-life wench who grinned from the bill-board to advertise somebody's toothpaste.

Like a little world of people drifting away into the depths of space, Athelstan Shelmerdine's torpedo-men and their burning car floated off into the night as I kept my foot down and zoomed up the highway like a highschool kid determined to kill himself or somebody else with his first hot-rod.

We didn't speak for a good five minutes. Then I put the headlights on again, and Joanne Kilvert said: 'That's Plymouth ahead.'

She was pointing to a string of lights on the horizon. The observation came in a matter-of-fact and deadpan way on the heels of what had just happened. She spoke like a guide pointing out the scenery rather than in the way of a woman who had lately been shot at.

I told myself that this slight, rain-bedraggled kid had guts. At that time I didn't know the half of it.

'That long story you mentioned, let me hear it,' I said. 'Those mugs are out of commission. You can tell me as we carry on to South Bend.'

She sat up in her seat, settled herself in with admirable coolness, considering what had just occurred, and began to preen rebel strands of hair with her fingers.

'I'm sorry I got you into this,' she began, and I marvelled in silence at the composure that now settled on her. No more trembling, in spite of her sodden clothes, no wide eyes and quivering mouth. She had self-control and guts all right, now that the immediate danger of the black coats and fedoras was over.

'Trouble is what I like, Miss Kilvert,' I said. 'Unfortunately, this is one time trouble caught me on the hop. I'm returning from a vacation and my heater

24

is with my sport clothes in the boot. I didn't figure I'd need it passing through Indiana.'

She smiled, vanquishing those hard lines that had shown on her face. I was glad they could be washed off with a single application of a smile. Hard lines on the face are for guys who live within smelling distance of the grubbier side of our civilisation — guys like me — for pretty girls still young enough to have voted in only one Presidential Election.

'Perhaps it was fate, meeting up with you,' Joanne Kilvert went on. 'I mean, I might have been given a ride by anybody who wouldn't have a notion what to do when those men showed up.' She was talking like a comic-strip heroine who was used to being chased and fired on as a matter of course.

I wasn't kidded. I remembered a scared little girl, anybody's kid-sister from anywhere at all, standing under a tree.

'They had you scared girlie,' I remarked. 'I give you credit for having guts, many a woman would still be in hysterics after that experience and many another would keep 'em up clear to South Bend. Give with the story.'

'I've had to have guts, the way I've been living for the past three months, Mr. Lantry.' The hint of those hard lines crept into her soft features again.

The lights of Plymouth grew bigger before us.

She gave with the story.

2

Joanne Kilvert had guts. The story she told me as we drove through Plymouth and on out towards South Bend proved that.

She got those transient lines of bitterness on her face the same way I got mine — living within smelling distance of the underworld. By the time South Bend showed up as a myriad scattering of lights on the far horizon, I had a great respect for the slight, dark-haired girl.

'My brother knew only too well who was behind the trade-union pushing in the Chicago region,' she said. 'It was the Shelmerdine organisation. Almost everybody knows that, the union men who are forced into giving a cut of their funds for protection; the politicians; the newspapers and the police. They all know, but they won't act. Athelstan Shelmerdine isn't just a man — he's a — a beast. You know how newspaper cartoonists draw something evil as an octopus with legs gripping a lot of people at the same time?'

I nodded.

'Well, that's what Athelstan Shelmerdine is. He's a monster. He has his tentacles stretching out all over the middle-west. He owns places and people at all levels; he can intimidate people into being his property, or he can buy them. When anyone offers resistance, or even looks dangerous, he can have them put out of the way . . . '

She paused. I suppose she was thinking of her brother, his wife and their baby. I took one hand off the wheel, fumbled in my pocket and found my packet of cigarettes and my lighter, gave her a cigarette and took one myself.

She puffed the cigarette into life gratefully.

'My brother was sick and tired of the undercover deals in his union. He was a fighter, Mr. Lantry. They gave him a medal for killing North Koreans when he was only a youngster. He thought he had a right to live in a clean and decent United States and he went out to fight corruption almost on his own, but he wasn't looking for another medal. All he wanted was a decent life for his family and himself. One or two of his supporters lost heart after a crowd of hoodlums beat them up. Arthur was beaten up too, but that only made him more determined. He began mentioning names. He produced a pamphlet on gangster interference in trade unionism and laid charges against big people who were corrupt to the core. You know what happened to him.'

'Sure, I know. The little man against the big combine. A lot of men tried what your brother tried, girlie. They had guts, but that's not enough when you're up against rotten and bribed officials. You need official support and you need to know that the official who's giving you the support is not buying his highballs and showing his girl a good time with money your enemies put in his pocket.'

'I was trained as a secretary,' went on Joanne Kilvert. 'I suppose I must have some of the same spirit Arthur had — I like to think I have. After my brother and his child were killed that day, by thugs who made a clear getaway, I was determined to do what I could about it. I knew Shelmerdine was behind the whole business and I knew, if I could only get something on him to place before the Crime Commission in Chicago, I might help to break him. He has a lot of front organisations; legitimate business concerns which cover his other activities. I managed to obtain a job with one of them, but I used a false name. Then, about three months back, Shelmerdine's personal secretary left him and I was recommended for the job. Maybe you can call it Providential. I quit the real estate agency which Shelmerdine owns as one of his above-board concerns and went to work out at his mansion. It's a big place just outside a town called Rollinsville — might as well call it Shelmerdinesville, because he seems to own the whole place.'

I grunted. I knew something of Shelmerdine by hearsay, he seemed to own sections of land and everyone in them like a cattle-baron of the Old West. It wasn't hard to think of him as an old-time *patrone* making everyone act when he hollered and running them off their holdings when they dared to raise a holler for themselves.

'This mansion of his,' continued Joanne Kilvert, 'is a fine old place in its own grounds. Shelmerdine lives like a king, but I always thought of him as a beast in a cave. It's a beautifully furnished cave where everything is veneered over. Shelmerdine has a wife, a quiet and pretty little woman who never asks any questions, and a small son of about six years. He's a family man. A big businessman who loves to spend all the time he can with his wife and child. I used to watch him play with the child on the lawn and I'd think of my brother and his child, buried in the ground, and my crippled sister-in-law.'

She took a long pull on the cigarette and I watched the lights of distant South Bend growing bigger.

A city, seen from a distance at night, is a fairyland of lights. It's hard to think that, among the lights, people are living out their lives; people are being born and other people are dying. It's hard to imagine that the far cluster of lights are a spangled cloak for the squalid things of the city; dirt, disease, strife and crime.

Joanne Kilvert went on: 'Everything at Shelmerdine's place was on the up-and-up. He rarely left home and conducted his businesses from there. Every letter I took down and typed was a legitimate business one, touching the affairs of Shelmerdine Enterprises Incorporated. No one ever used gangster talk, no one ever produced a gun. There was no poker playing in smoky rooms, no whisky bottles strewn about the place. There were no gangsters' molls and nobody ever tried to paw me. I had my own suite of rooms and I was treated with respect and paid well. There were no mobster types about the place, but there was no disguising what the two chauffeurs, the gardener and his helper and even the butler, with what he thought was an English accent, really were. There were also a couple of uniformed men who prowled about the grounds to keep out intruders. There was a very studied and very obvious gloss of respectability about the place, Mr. Lantry, but I wasn't fooled.'

She paused to stub out the butt of her cigarette in the ashtray on the dashboard.

'I know the kind of set-up,' I told her. 'I've been in some joints that were built with dirty money myself. I bet you could smell the rotgut booze Shelmerdine peddled in the 'twenties. Maybe, if you were extra-sensitive, you caught the echo of a machine-gun coming from a Chicago back-alley thirty years in the past every time you glanced at Shelmerdine's art treasures.'

'No,' she answered. 'I wasn't interested in how Athelstan Shelmerdine made his money. I was only concerned with what he had done to people near to me.'

'And hundreds of other people, all of them near to somebody,' I said.

'He began to trust me with a great deal of work out of the usual run of a secretary's job. Pretty soon, I had the run of his office and the keys to his safe. I only saw the business side of Shelmerdine's life, of course, and he was always the perfect gentleman. Once in a while, men he called 'business associates' would call and he'd have private conversations with them. They always looked like businessmen on the surface, but I could sense what they were under the business suits.'

I smiled to myself. I would have used the word 'smell'.

'I got my chance when Shelmerdine was off on one of his business trips,' she continued. 'I was alone in the office and I searched the safe. There was a compartment which I never had occasion to open, but I found the key to it on the key-ring and found it chock-full of papers. They concerned Shelmerdine's other business deals — his real business. They touched on everything, dope, drugs, vice, trade union protection; there were names and dates that would pull down Shelmerdine and a lot of other people if I could only give those papers to the Crime Commission. I had the means of wrecking Shelmerdine and his whole organisation in my hands. I locked the papers up again. I had to think it out and plan my moves.

'I knew Shelmerdine would soon be back, but he was to go on a longer trip later to-day, that is — if I waited, I would stand a better chance of getting clear. I packed my grip a full week before, perhaps I betrayed myself in some way, I don't know. Anyway, Ike Tescachelli, the senior chauffeur, began to watch me in a way I didn't like. I thought perhaps he had found out about my true identity and was suspicious, then again he might simply have been looking out for a chance to get fresh when the big boss was away.'

I remembered the Italian-looking hood who spoke to me at the mouth of the dirt road.

'Ike Tescachelli, is he the one with the small moustache?' I asked.

'Yes. He usually stays close to Shelmerdine and drives him around, but Greg Cortines, the second chauffeur, went with him on this trip. Tescachelli had his eye on me for two or three days and I was worried. As soon as Shelmerdine set off on his trip, I opened the safe and took the papers. I stuffed them into my grip and I was ready to run for it. I had already checked the bus time-table and knew I could get a bus into South Bend once I was on the main highway and I could take a train or bus to Chicago from South Bend.

'I had a story ready in case anyone questioned me and I slipped out of a side door. I was about to leave the grounds of the house by a small gate leading into a back road when one of the gardeners appeared and asked me where I was going. I told him I was taking a walk into Rollinsville to have the clasp of my grip repaired and he seemed to believe me. I was clear of the house when I realised the awful mistake I had made. In my haste, I left the key in the lock of the safe after locking it. It might go unnoticed until Shelmerdine returned, but it was sure to give away the fact that I had tampered with the safe — and I'd been seen leaving with a grip.'

She paused for a moment to catch her breath, as though at the recollection of that chilling moment when she realised how she had betrayed herself.

The coupe passed a South Bend city

36

limits sign; the glare of the city was closer now and it brought a certain warmth. It was like coming to a place of friendly men after being in the dark outlands for too long.

'I panicked, Mr. Lantry,' went on the girl. 'I ran for it, trying to get to the highway as quickly as I could. I didn't know my way around very well and I took a couple of wrong turnings. By the time I did reach the highway, I was just in time to see the bus I wanted sailing away into the distance. I was terribly scared. I just kept walking, then an old farmer in an old-fashioned truck picked me up and gave me a lift to the other side of Peru and I kept on walking after that, even when the rain started.'

'Then I picked you up, huh,' I grunted, 'and you still have those documents in the grip? No, that's a silly question. It's obvious that you have, you've been clinging to your baggage as though it'll leave you a fortune when it dies.'

I watched South Bend growing bigger before us and I was worried.

I couldn't leave this little chick to run

about the countryside with Athelstan Shelmerdine's strong-arms on her tail.

'You intend to hand the papers to the Crime Commission in Chicago?' I asked. She nodded and I fell to musing out loud. 'And Shelmerdine pulls almost every string that's pullable in Chicago; if his outfit knows you're in the Windy City, they'll serve up the table d'hote pretty damn quick — with you as the dish. Where will you go, once you've succeeded in putting the papers in the hands of the crime-chasers, I mean?'

'Why, home. My parents live out at Woodstock.'

I thought about that for a while. Woodstock was close to Chicago and Shelmerdine's hired hands might track the girl out there.

'Does Shelmerdine and his crowd know you hail from the Chicago area?'

'Yes, but nobody at Shelmerdine's country house knows my home address and they think my name is Maybelle Jones.'

'But they'll probably figure you'll head for Chicago, since that's your home-town.

It's my guess that our friends who had the mishap in the sedan were chasing you because they realised you'd blown with something out of the safe and they wanted you back — and whatever you'd taken — before Shelmerdine got back from his trip. It was desperate and ham-fisted. That business of opening fire on a state highway proves it. Shelmerdine left that sort of stuff behind him with prohibition. When he wants shooting done in public, he hires gutter-rats like those who killed your brother to do it; his kind of smooth mobster doesn't allow those who are close to him to charge around the country blasting away with heaters — it's bringing the dirt too close to his own doorstep. The real chase, girlie, the top-shelf subtle stuff, will come when big-shot Athelstan gets back and finds out just what's missing from the safe.'

She tried to stifle a sneeze by pressing a slender forefinger to her top lip. It escaped her clutches.

The sneeze decided me on a half-formed plan that had been floating about my mind.

39

'Listen,' I told her. 'You've been soaked to the skin and you've had a rough time. You need rest and dry clothing. I'm on my way to visit some old friends in South Bend and you stay right with me. These folk are great — an old army pal and his wife — they'll fix you a place for the night and the strong-arm hoodlums will never think of looking for you in South Bend. Tomorrow, we'll push on to Chicago. Meantime, I'll get in touch with my branch in Chicago to stand by for some action. World Wide Investigations will back you up, girlie. You deserve somebody on your side and, besides, I have an interest in this fight — those bums fired bullets into my car. Deal?'

She nodded her approval while stifling another sneeze.

So, we drove into South Bend and into the realisation that it was Saturday night. I jockeyed the car along the wide sweep of Michigan Street with its bright sky-signs and its trees. The movies were disgorging their patrons at that hour. There was a bustle of activity on the street, still glossed by recent rain.

I drove steadily through the mass of cars. It was my first time in South Bend for some years, but I remembered my way around. On the way up from the south, I had reflected pleasantly on how surprised Jack and Beth Kay would be at my unexpected visit. Now I was calling on them with a total stranger but, what the heck, Jack and Beth were friendly, happy-go-lucky people, they'd make us both welcome.

I could book a couple of rooms at a hotel, but the Kays would be highly insulted if I stayed in South Bend without making use of their high, wide and handsome hospitality. That's the kind of folk Jack and Beth were. Good folk.

It's comforting to think that the world holds more of their kind than the other species.

Cautiously, I drove along Michigan with its bright lights and glittering theatre awnings, waited dutifully at the intersection of Munroe Street until the traffic cop signalled me across. I took the coupe easily though the tangle of crossings at mid-Michigan Street and on up to the

41

bridge spanning the St. Joseph river then over the river to Leeper Avenue.

It was quiet and residential. The buildings of the University of Notre Dame stood not too far away, a stately group against the summer night sky with a church spire and a great golden dome dominant.

I glanced at Joanne Kilvert. She had been very quiet for a long time.

She was sound asleep. Just like a kid.

I drove along steadily with one eye on the neat painted houses. I remembered Jack's place vaguely but recognised the house as soon as the headlight beams picked it out. A pang of something, maybe envy, hit me as I saw the trim house and its neat lawn.

It looked like it belonged to somebody and somebody belonged to it.

Why the hell didn't I have a comfortable house, a nice wife and a nine to six job? Settling down would be great.

I hit the brakes, shaking off the feeling with the action.

I had no squawks coming. I had wanted to be a private dick. From starting out in a back room, I'd wound up with a world wide investigation outfit. I didn't want to be another solid citizen. I already was what I wanted to be — a shamus, but a shamus *par excellence*, I hoped.

The jerk of the brakes wakened Joanne. She sat up quickly and looked about in slight alarm.

'Relax. You're with friends,' I told her as I stepped out of the car.

The sidewalk was still wet after the rain. There was a fresh scent from the nearby trees.

I walked up the pathway, mounted the three or four steps to the Kays' porch and hit the doorbell. Deep in the soul of the house there was a buzz which ceased when I took my thumb from the bell-push.

Through the frosted glass of the door I saw a bloom of light as someone opened a door in the interior of the house. The bulk of a figure loomed against the light and a light illuminated the hallway as a switch snapped. The door opened and Jack Kay stood there, blocky, with a crew-cut and wearing the kind of clothes a man can loaf around in. There were house slippers on his feet.

'Tear yourself away from that television set, you're entertaining to-night,' I said. There was a hollowness to the words, the joviality was forced. I wasn't sure I was doing the right thing in bringing Joanne here.

Jack Kay's features settled into a wide grin of surprise and he hit me a playful blow in the stomach.

'Lantry, you old scoundrel! Come in!'

I jerked my thumb towards the coupe standing at the kerb.

'I have somebody with me — a girl.'

Jack put his hands on his hips and looked at me steadily.

'I detect a certain furtive tone,' he said. 'Can it be that you finally got married and are suffering from henpeck malady? Or are you eloping with somebody?'

I grinned at Jack's easy-going joshing. This was him all over.

'Look, Jack, this is to do with a case,' I confided. 'It's something I got into by accident when I was driving up from Florida. I was on my way to see you anyway, but I gave this kid a ride and found she's on the run from Athelstan Shelmerdine's mob. She wasn't one of his crowd — don't get that idea; she's been doing some slick detective work on her own. She's the sister of Kilvert, the guy who was killed in Chicago some time back.'

'Arthur Kilvert, the trade union guy?'

I nodded.

'She has something on the Shelmerdine crowd that can break them for keeps, that's why she's on the lam.' I went on to give him a quick outline of the story behind Joanne Kilvert. Jack gave a low whistle of surprise. 'Right now, she's about all in. Maybe a spell with decent folks in respectable surroundings will help her along. She's got guts and she's held out well, but she's weary and she's been soaked to the skin.'

'Well, bring her in,' he invited. 'You know us. Our friends and friends of our friends always welcome,' he turned towards the hallway and bellowed: 'Hey, Beth. It's Mike Lantry and a friend. Break out the coffee-pot!'

I heard a squeak of surprise from Beth, somewhere deep in the house, as I walked down the pathway towards the car.

I brought Joanne Kilvert back along the walk. Beth Kay, slim and dark, was standing in the doorway with her husband.

'Long time no see,' she called cheerfully to me.

Joanne Kilvert was shy and self-conscious, trying to smooth out the creases in her rain-stained skirt and straighten the crumpled jacket of her summer costume.

Also, she had the sniffles.

I introduced everybody. Joanne was still a little troubled. I guess Jack must have given Beth a very brief and whispered outline of the set-up while I was helping the girl out of the car for she put Joanne at ease at once in her matter-of-fact way.

'Cold coming,' she observed. 'Hot bath is what you need, honey, then some hot coffee. Finest cure in the world.' Beth put her arm around Joanne's waist and shepherded her into the house. I was glad to see the girl afforded this womanish tenderness, it would help a lot after my own ham-fisted way of dealing with the damsel in distress.

Jack ushered me into the lounge while the two disappeared upstairs. He settled me on the davenport, produced scotch and glasses and fisted a generous drink into my hand.

'So you're fighting the Shelmerdine organisation,' he murmured as he seated himself in an easy chair. 'It's a big team to lick, Mike.'

'I know it,' I replied. 'I got into this by accident, Jack, but if ever anyone needed backing up it's that kid. I'll stick close by her until I can get her to safety where the Shelmerdine crowd can't hurt her or her folks. I'm putting my Chicago office on to this Shelmerdine guy — we'll get those papers into the hands of the Crime Commission and I'm sticking around the mid-west until we do.'

'Where do you intend sending the girl?' he asked. 'Anywhere within a big radius of Chicago will hardly be safe with the Shelmerdine organisation on her tail.'

'I half thought of New York — yes, I

think I'll put her on a train for New York to-morrow and 'phone Lucy, my secretary, to meet her and look after her for a while. In fact, I'll put a call through from here to Lucy's apartment and one to Walt Toland, my Chicago agency chief. I'll tip Walton off about this set-up and put those papers the girl took in the mail to him as soon as I can. I guess the U.S. Mail is as safe a place as anywhere for documents as red hot as those.'

Jack's face clouded. He shook his head gloomily.

'Sorry about the 'phone — it's kaput. We had a freak storm here this evening and lightning hit the power-line for this whole neighbourhood, I guess every 'phone in this section of the city is out of action.'

I grunted.

'I guess it'll keep until to-morrow, I'll use a public telephone somewhere around the city.'

Beth came into the room.

'Your protegee is wallowing in hot water . . . ' she began.

'You can say that again,' I cut in with

an attempt at humour.

'Scat!' said Beth. 'She's wallowing in hot water and she tells me she has a change of dress in her grip out in the car. Don't sit around drinking whisky, go get her grip — and put your car in the garage while you're about it.'

I jumped, remembering the grip with those incriminating papers out in the car. Although Joanne had clutched hold of that grip as though it owed her money previously, I guessed her good manners jibbed at walking into the house of total strangers with it in her hand.

I went out quickly, took the car into Jack's garage and removed my own grip from the boot, taking it back to the house with Joanne Kilvert's.

Beth took the girl's baggage and hastened upstairs with it.

I joined Jack again and finished my drink.

Beth reappeared, ducked into the kitchen and, in a remarkably short time, was hollering for us to come and get it.

Jack and I settled ourselves down at a laden table that looked and smelled pretty good. I'd forgotten how hungry I was.

Joanne appeared in the doorway, shyly. She was wearing a wide skirted summer dress, her hair had been smoothed neatly. There were no lines of bitterness on her face now and her gently moulded features were touched with a judicious amount of cosmetic.

She looked mighty good.

In spite of her sniffles.

'Wade into supper,' invited Beth, 'and we'll be in time to catch the late night epic on TV.'

I stretched lazily.

'Ah, civilised American life,' I said.

3

Beth settled Joanne into the spare bedroom right after the TV show.

Jack did something to a hidden button on the davenport and it promptly turned into a bed.

'For putting up folk when you're overcrowded,' he explained. Beth came from somewhere or other with an armful of blankets and pillows. She began clothing the nakedness of the newly created bed in her matter-of-fact way.

'This is where you sleep, Lantry,' she informed me. 'You're nearest the kitchen, so you make coffee for everyone first thing in the morning.'

And I did.

The sun was shining brightly and South Bend's church bells reminded me it was Sunday morning. I pottered around the electric cooker, making coffee, listening to the distant bells and a nearer one clanging across from the

University campus.

Just being there, I felt that nag of something again. Was it envy?

With the coffee made, I progressed to the foot of the stairs.

'Coffee ready,' I bellowed. 'Come down and get — I'm not bringing it up!'

A disgruntled remark in Jack's tones floated down.

He was the first to appear, unshaven and very much the average man on Sunday morning. The girls came down after we'd finished off two cups of coffee and a cigarette each. Neither of them would show herself before going through the rituals that would remove the first-thing-in-the-morning appearance.

We breakfasted and I shaved, then we held a council as to what should be done with Joanne. Without any trouble at all, I sold her the idea that she would be safe with Lucy in New York and I decided on going out to find out what time there was a train for New York that day, also to find a telephone in working order to call Walt Toland in Chicago and Lucy in New York.

Jack offered to drive me to the Union Depot, but I settled for his instructions on how to reach it.

I took the car out of the garage after examining the bullet-holes in the back. Two of them close together, near to the right rear wing. Those hoods must have been aiming for the tyre and they came damned near to hitting it.

I took it easy driving down into the centre of the city. One or two Sunday drivers were just getting started, but there was no appreciable rush of traffic on the roads.

There was a nice feeling of this being a city on its day off. People came out of churches; people stood talking at street corners; the factory smoke-stacks over to the south of the city were lifeless.

I found West South Street and the Union Depot without much trouble, parked the coupe and made enquiries. There was a train for New York that very afternoon, which was great. There was a telephone booth on the station, which was also great.

I called Walt Toland, using his home

number, knowing he would not be at the agency on Sunday.

'Hi, Walt. Lantry.'

A gurgle of surprise came from Walt's end; maybe he was taking the call from his bed.

'I'm in South Bend, Walt, with something pretty big. I have some papers here that mean curtains for the Athelstan Shelmerdine organisation once they get into the hands of the Crime Commission. I'm putting them in the mail for you first thing to-morrow. This being Sunday, the post offices are all closed and I want to put this package in express delivery.'

'But, if you're only in South Bend, why not bring them up here to-day? You can be in Chicago in a couple of hours.'

'No,' I said. 'I'll trust the mail. I'm sticking around Indiana for a while.'

The truth was, I had already decided to do some mooching around the vicinity of Shelmerdine's country mansion and Rollinsville, once I had put the girl safely on the New York train.

Put it down to my being toned up too high a degree after my Florida vacation;

or put it down to the Lantry weakness for sticking his neck out.

'Okay,' agreed Walt's voice. 'You want me to give these papers to the Crime Commission as soon as I get them?'

'As soon as you get them Walt. I'll address the package to you personally. This is hush-hush, understand? There's nothing in this for anybody's eyes but World Wide's and the Crime Commission's. No tip-offs for the newspapers. Keep it hushed up and it'll go off like a hydrogen bomb, shaking all kinds of bribed big-shots from their money-lined rat-holes.'

'Right, chief,' said Walt. He must have sensed I was about to stick my neck out, he added: 'Luck!'

'Luck to you,' I said. Which concluded the call.

Next I called Lucy's apartment after waiting for quite a time while the long-distance call was put through.

Lucy answered the 'phone grouchily, as though I had disrupted her late Sunday breakfast, but she brightened when she heard who the caller was.

I told her what time to meet the train and gave a description of Joanne.

'Make her at home for a while,' I told her. 'If she's bored, she can give you a hand at the office. She's a secretary and this is one who is really efficient.'

An indignant splutter came from Lucy's end.

'Relax, Lucy,' I grinned. 'Your pedestal isn't in danger. But, seriously, look after the kid, huh?'

'Certainly, Mr. Lantry. Depend on me.'

'Good girl. See you around.'

I walked out of the booth and out to the street, climbed in the coupe and started back for the Kays' place. It was still a pleasant Sunday morning and I enjoyed the drive.

Joanne was giving Beth a hand with lunch when I arrived and Jack was knee-deep in the Sunday editions. It was all so cosy and family-ish that I had to guard like all hell against that feeling of envy that was so good at getting through the chinks in my armour.

I told Joanne there was a train that afternoon and that her future for the next few weeks would be a bright one. She went upstairs and returned with her ready-packed grip in one hand and a small package wrapped in brown paper in the other.

She handed me the package. Such a small thing; but so damned important it was like taking hold of radium.

'Just handing it over to someone is like taking a heavy weight off my back,' Joanne admitted.

I stowed the package inside my jacket. In doing so, my jacket flipped open a little too wide, revealing the shoulder holster and the 9 mm Browning I had strapped on that morning.

Joanne didn't see it, she was *en route* to the kitchen to continue helping out with lunch. Jack didn't see it, either, he was snorting over the opinions of some sports-writer in the paper he was reading.

I felt myself blush to the roots of my hair, just the same.

Carrying a gun in the home of a friend!

I sat down and tried to cover my discomfort by reading the comic section.

A car snorted to a halt out on the

street, close to the house.

Two seconds passed.

The doorbell sounded.

'I'll get it,' said Jack.

He went through to the hallway. I heard him open the door, heard him give an odd gasp. Then there was a confused scuffle of brief duration, somebody said something dirty and Jack was backing into the lounge.

Forcing him back, were three men. Three men in black coats and soft fedoras, with that certain sameness about them.

Their guns were all alike, too.

Ike Tescachelli was to the fore, jabbing the mouth of his heater into Jack's midriff.

A gasp sounded from the door which gave on to the kitchen.

Beth and Joanne were standing there, wide-eyed and faces drained of colour.

I moved for the Browning under my jacket, but it was a vain hope and I knew it.

'Uh-uh,' said Tescachelli of the clipped moustache, waving his automatic as

58

though cautioning a child.

He was right, of course, so I uh-uhed and left my Browning in its cosy bed.

In back of my skull, what brains I have were ticking over like O'Toole's heart the day somebody kidded him the Irish Republic was going dry.

How in all the shades of hell had these bums tracked us down to Jack's house? It must have been the car, my car standing outside that railroad depot. Shelmerdine must have put all his bulldogs out and this bunch must have been prowling around South Bend. They'd remembered the car and the bullet scars on it would clinch it. They must have followed me and I never knew it. No more vacations in Florida for me. The sun slowed me up so I didn't even notice when I was being tailed.

Mr. Ike Tescachelli chose to drop a few verbal pearls.

'Stand still, all of you,' he growled in a voice that sounded like somebody marching over a couple of thousand eggs in GI boots. 'Stand still and nobody gets hurt. We want the papers that were taken from

59

Mr. Shelmerdine's safe — and we want you, Miss Jones.' His verbal pearls were dropped in the direction of Joanne, standing in a frozen attitude next to Beth, in the portal of the kitchen.

Jack was standing closer to the hoods than I was, obviously itching to take a few swings at them, but using his common-sense in the face of the plethora of heaters.

What riled me was the way this had suddenly happened in the Kay's house. Like I had dragged a lump of my crummy edge-of-the-underworld life under their decent roof.

'Where,' asked Tescachelli, 'are those papers, Miss Jones?'

Joanne stood stock still, white faced, but keeping her mouth closed.

I took a step forward, moving closer to the Shelmerdine hoods.

'Look,' I said, 'you can't walk into a person's house with — '

'Shaddap,' said Tescachelli.

' — guns drawn, threatening people this way. It's an offence.' I was playing the hick again.

'Shaddap,' said Tescachelli again. 'I don't know who you are, Mac, but I don't like you.' He turned towards Joanne. 'Now where are those papers?'

No reply. One of the hoods, taller than the others and with a lean and hungry look that would have made J. Caesar flip his wig, licked his lips.

'Maybe she's got 'em on her, Ike. Should I frisk her?'

'Shaddap. Shaddap,' rasped Tescachelli twice more. It sounded like somebody ripping sailcloth. He made a move towards Joanne, then stopped short when he spotted her grip standing where she had placed it on the floor. He gave Joanne a sharp glance with those fine, dark Italian eyes. He said: 'So, you won't talk, huh!' which reminded me of a 1930 gangster movie all over again. Tescachelli nodded to lean and hungry Cassius. 'That's her grip, Slats, take a look in it. If we don't get those papers quick, we get rough.'

Cassius took a couple of steps towards the grip and bent over it.

'It's locked,' he reported.

Tescachelli was watching him, the third mug, a small, pockmarked man, was watching Jack Kay, but half his interest was with Cassius, fiddling with the grip.

I moved for my gun again.

But I underestimated Ike Tescachelli. I was near enough to him for him to swipe out at me with the flat of his automatic. Which he did.

He caught my movement with the corner of his eye and hit me a hell of a crack across the mouth, so hard that I crumpled and hit the deck. I lay there, seeing stars, like an injured comic-strip character. I could feel the impression of the gun around my teeth and my mouth seemed to be full of brine.

'Take that heater off him, Slats,' said Tescachelli's voice from beyond the galaxy of stars.

Hands began to fumble around with me and there was a hoarse yip of surprise.

'Hey, Ike, there's a package here, in his inside pocket,' said the voice of the lean hungry one. There was a movement around the region of my inner coat pocket. That Cassius was dumb as a stuffed owl. He took the package, but forgot about my Browning. I could feel the weight of it, resting comfortably against the upper part of my ribs.

The fourth of July firework display cleared and I opened my eyes, raising my head a little. There was a drooling wetness creeping from the corner of my mouth.

Tescachelli was opening the package. Slats was standing close to him, looking like an overgrown puppy expecting sugar for bringing back the stick his master had thrown. Pock-marks was watching Jack with his gun levelled and Jack was watching Pock-marks with his fists bundled up. Beth and Joanne were still two pallid waxworks in the kitchen doorway.

'It's them,' Tescachelli said as he examined the papers. 'Grab the girl and let's go.'

'What about him?' asked Slats, nodding towards me.

'The hell with him,' growled Tescachelli. 'Mr. Shelmerdine said he wanted the papers and the girl and that's what we're bringing him.'

Tescachelli grabbed hold of Joanne and hoisted her towards the door giving on to the hall, Slats and Pock-marks followed him as he hauled her out. The little guy with the pock-marks was the last one through the door — almost.

I guess Jack Kay couldn't contain himself any longer, he grabbed the little hood by the shoulder with one hand, hauled him around and planted his other fist into Pock-marks' mouth with a satisfying meaty sound.

Pock-marks staggered back and hit the door-jamb. He still had his heater in his hand. Behind him, in the hall, the sound of his buddies opening the street door echoed.

He was half-slumped against the door-jamb. The automatic came up like lightning. I saw Jack, only a matter of a yard or so away from the Shelmerdine mobster, pitch himself quickly to one side just as the gun bellowed. Jack went scooting backwards, holding his left arm and coming to rest against the further wall.

I heard Beth scream, another world away.

Pock-marks was bringing his gun up towards Jack again. This time, it was for the kill.

I didn't think anybody, leave alone a half-dazed somebody like I was right then, could roll over from his back to his belly, pull a gun from his shoulder-holster and fire as fast as I did.

What's more, I hit Pock-marks twice and he never got around to pulling the trigger on Jack.

He stood on buckled knees, leaning against the door-jamb, looking at me with wide-eyed wonderment as the gun fell from his grasp.

Jack was panting against the wall, clutching his injured arm.

Beth was hiding her face against the jamb of the kitchen door. There was no sound from the remaining two Shelmerdine men and Joanne. I guessed they were clear of the house by now, and the sound of the shooting was not enticing them back.

Pock-marks decided to take leave of us.

He swivelled about and made for the door on wobbly legs. He was still wearing that expression of wonderment, reminiscent of that you find on the faces of little kids on Christmas morning.

I watched him go as I picked myself up. I didn't give him long odds on getting far. He staggered out into the hall. I went after him at a short distance, holding the Browning. I wasn't notably steady on my own legs.

The street door was open and Pock-marks was making for it. I could see a big Cadillac down at the kerb, just beginning to creep away. Dimly, I saw Slats in the back of the car, with his hand over Joanne's mouth. Tescachelli was driving. The shooting must have panicked him and he wasn't waiting for the wounded man.

Pock-marks made the porch, he began waving a feeble hand at the departing Cadillac, mouthing something. Maybe he was telling his pals good-bye. He made the first couple of steps. Then the next two.

The Cadillac shot away from the kerb as though panicked out of its creeping by the staggering, mouthing man trying to

66

reach it. Pock-marks kept on wobbling along the path, lost his way and went teetering across the lawn like a skid-row rummy who had just killed a bottle.

He stiffened, gurgled and fell face first into the centre of the lawn. My only regret was that he hadn't made it to the gutter to die — preferably a gutter a long way from the Kay home.

I didn't even want to go and examine the corpse. I felt cheap and dirty right through. With my stupidity in coming here with the girl, I had brought this unsavoury incident to the home of two fine people.

Now, there was the stiff of a grubby little crook out on their front lawn. And the Shelmerdine crowd had both the girl and the papers.

I needed someone to give me a swift kick in the rear.

Back in the house, Beth was attending to Jack's arm. The slug had passed right through the fleshy part of the upper arm.

'I'm sorry,' I began, speaking with difficulty because of the swipe across the mouth Tescachelli had handed me with his gun. 'I'm sorry I had to bring this under your roof. I've been a fool. Those crumbs must have been prowling around town when I was down at the depot. They must have seen my car and followed me . . . '

'Don't apologise,' said Jack. 'I'll get me a gun and go after those bums with you!'

'No,' I said. 'These aren't the old days, Jack. We aren't a couple of kids carrying rifles after Patton any more. You have Beth now and that arm needs a doctor's attention. Besides, the cops will be along here any minute. That shooting brought one or two of your neighbours out on to the street. Act dumb, Jack, tell them I turned up with a girl named Joanne. Tell them you don't know her other name and don't mention Shelmerdine's name or those papers. Those hoods burst in here, snatched the girl, shot at you when you offered resistance and I shot that character out on the lawn. Neither you nor Beth know what it's all about.'

'Okay,' Jack agreed reluctantly.

I fumbled in my pocket, found a scrap of paper and wrote the telephone number of the Chicago branch of World Wide Investigations on it, and then Walt Toland's home number.

'If you don't hear from me in about six hours, ring either one of these numbers and ask for Walt Toland. Tell Walt I've gone out to the Shelmerdine mansion near Rollinsville and it looks like I'm in trouble. Tell him the deal I spoke to him about this morning has blown sky high and he'd better come running with some of his boys.'

'Check,' grunted Jack, 'but I still think I should come with you.'

'No soap,' I said. 'I'll hate myself for the rest of my days for what's happened here to-day.'

I made for the hallway. I still felt like the lowest form of life on earth and my injured mouth felt about four times too big.

'Good luck,' said Jack to my back.

'Good luck,' echoed Beth, 'and get that kid away from them, Mike.'

I went down all the porch steps at one hop.

Pock-marks was still sprawling on the

lawn and quite a little crowd of people was standing on the side-walk. I ignored them all, thinking only of Joanne in the hands of the Shelmerdine organisation. I got the coupe out of the garage in nothing flat and was nosing it off the drive on to the street when a cop appeared. He was only a kid and a good physical example of South Bend's beat-pounders. I bet it was the first time he ever had a stiff on his beat.

He stepped up to the car, looking unsure of what he should do.

I fished in my pocket and flashed my badge before he could speak.

'Investigator. World Wide. I'm Lantry, the head of the outfit and I shot that guy because he shot a pal of mine,' I told him.

He opened and closed his mouth a couple of times, like a codfish trying to pluck up courage to propose to a lady codfish. He got it out at last: 'I'll have to ask you to stay. This is very irregular. Homicide will want — '

'I'll talk to homicide when I have the time,' I told him, 'right now, I'm in the biggest hurry I was ever in.'

I warmed up the coupe and took off under his nose.

I guess he played the codfish some more, because I proceeded to break the speed limit, also under his nose.

4

I kept on breaking the speed limit for quite a distance, until I was over the bridge and heading for the centre of the city. As I kept going south through the Sunday-tranquil city, I expected to hear the wail of a police siren behind me at any minute.

It never came.

Thanks to that freak storm, Codfish the Cop must have had trouble in getting into telephonic communication with the station-house. There was no sense in kidding myself. Every cop in South Bend would be on the look out for me pretty damn quick once the events at the Kay house set the flatfoot machine ticking over.

So, I kept on going south. Somewhere on that highway was the big Cadillac with Tescachelli, Cassius, and, most important of all on the passenger-list, Joanne Kilvert. They would head for Shelmerdine's country place, for sure, and I had only a vague idea that it was somewhere near Rollingsville and that Rollingsville was somewhere beyond Peru. But I'd find it.

Out beyond the city limits I went, hitting a smart lick, despite the clutter of Sunday drivers here and there.

My mouth still hurt where it had made the acquaintance of Ike Tescachelli's gun. I began to wonder why I hadn't taken up some other way of earning a living, like selling insurance or painting fences.

Well clear of the city, I still saw nothing of the Cadillac. The five-day-a-week insurance salesmen and fence-painters, taking their wives and kids out for a Sunday ride, flashed past me on the left hand lane of the highway, streaked before me and in my own lane. I was one of a line of drivers, only they were looking for a summer afternoon's relaxation while I was looking for two hoods and a girl.

I began to curse Sunday drivers.

For no real reason, I hit the switch of the car radio. Some female crooner who I wouldn't have paid in chewing-gum wrappers wailed out of the radio grille dismally. The background band wasn't too good, either. It sounded like it was trying beat the wailing woman to the final fullstop on the music copy and it was winning by a couple of heads.

The band and the woman never finished out the race. They faded out as though someone had decided to put them, and the radio audience, out of their misery. A crisp voice said:

'Station WSBT, South Bend, Indiana. Attention. South Bend police are searching for Mike Lantry, of New York, in connection with a shooting in the city at mid-day to-day. Lantry is believed to be driving a red and cream 1956 drophead coupe and was last seen heading south in the direction of the centre. He is aged about thirty, wearing a lightweight sharkskin suit of grey, is hatless, has slightly curly dark hair and a scar on the left cheek. If sighted, please notify Police Department, South Bend, or nearest city or state police officer.'

I began to swear like a marine sergeant, while the wailing woman and the band returned. Anyone who had bets placed on the previous race would be pretty sore, they had finished it while the announcer was saying his piece and were now getting into a new number. It seemed to me the woman stood a good chance of winning this one, but I wasn't greatly interested.

That description of me was a good one. It came from Codfish the Cop, without a doubt. He was the last one to get a real good look at me and he'd seen me heading south for the city centre.

He hadn't taken my registration number, though, so they wouldn't make him a sergeant yet awhile. That description had me worried. I wondered how many of the Sunday drivers around me had picked it up. Then, there were the highway patrol cops to worry about.

The woman on the radio began to wail 'Nobody Knows de Trouble I Seen' which was just about the last straw, so I killed the singer and the band with a flick of the switch.

I kept on going, keeping my head slightly down over the wheel.

Somebody, or something, must have been on my side. I didn't see anything of the Cadillac, but none of the other drivers showed any signs of interest in me or my car. There were a lot of cars like mine around, which was something to be grateful for.

The luck deserted me a little way before I reached Plymouth.

I ran out of gas. Just like that.

Fuming, I pulled into the side of the highway, remembering that the last time I fuelled up was on the drive up from the south, long before I picked up Joanne Kilvert.

The insurance salesmen and the fence-painters continued to flash by, but a big long-distance truck came snorting up with a blue plume of exhaust spouting from the pipe above the cab. It shuddered to a stop and the trucker came down out of the cab, a big fellow in oily jeans and a sweaty T-shirt, open to show the world that he had somehow appropriated half the Brazilian jungle and was successfully growing it on his chest.

I thought maybe he'd heard that broadcast and spotted my car, but he gave me an affable grin.

'Out of gas, Mac?' he asked.

'Yes,' I told him.

'Gas station a little ways up the road. I have to call there to make a 'phone call. I can give you a ride so you can buy a can. You don't have far to walk back.'

'That's big of you,' said I, a little distrustful of him. I got out of the car and walked towards the truck. The big guy walked beside me.

I climbed up to the seat next to the driver's. The cab smelt oily and it chugged and rattled to the thrumming of the heavy engine, making Marilyn Monroe, cut from a magazine and pinned above the windshield, perform a jittery dance.

'Don't like to see a guy stranded without gas,' said the Samaritan as he hoisted himself into his seat. 'Happened to me too many times.'

I was still dubious of him. Also, I didn't like the idea of leaving my radio-publicised car standing by the edge of the highway while I went to the service station.

'Must be a trying job on occasion, yours,' I observed as he put the truck into motion.

'Yeah, it's that, all right,' said Jungle-chest. 'It gets real tryin' at times.'

'D'you have a radio in the cab to make things less boring?' I asked.

He snorted. 'The lousy outfit I'm workin' for don't provide no radios. They can't even give a guy his correct delivery instructions. I trucked out of South Bend with a load for Kokomo and I just now discovered my papers cover an entirely different load for Shreveport. Imagine that.'

I imagined it, but was too relieved at finding the truck had no radio to have much sympathy.

'Big fuss in South Bend,' said Jungle-chest, out of the blue. 'Guy got shot, it seems.'

'Yeah?'

'Yeah. Up near the University campus. In broad daylight, too.'

'What d'you know?' I said, as though I wasn't particularly interested.

I changed the subject quickly. 'How do I get to Rollinsville?'

'What do you want in a hick town like Rollinsville?' he asked. 'Last place God made.'

'Looking up my wife's Aunt Anastasia since I'm passing through this part of the country,' I lied.

'Uh-huh. You go through Plymouth and keep on until you hit a side-road running off the highway just before Peru. That'll take you into Uffotsberg, the second last place God made, and Rollinsville is the next town you hit.'

He pulled the truck to a snorting stop. We were at the gas station, a clutter of white buildings and gasoline pumps. We stepped down into the sunshine and the mingled smell of gas, oil and sun-beaten asphalt.

In the larger of the buildings, there was a counter, littered with equipment. A round faced, sleepy looking character, whom Jungle-chest addressed as 'Al', was leaning on the far side of the counter, looking like an impassive moon floating over the ocean of tools.

I wondered whether Al had heard that radio flash, but he looked as though he hadn't even heard who won the 1948 Presidential Election yet. He didn't open his eyes more than half way while I bought a can of gasoline from him.

In the background, the truck driver was bellowing into an old-fashioned wall telephone. He was telling someone named Carl about having the wrong delivery papers. I paid Al and he closed his eyes the full distance to go into his doze again.

'Thanks for the help,' I called to Jungle-chest.

'Y'wanna waken up that office staff, Carl — okay, Mac, y'welcome. Hate to see a guy stranded without gas. Yeah, I know it ain't all your fault, Carl, but, hell, I should have had to-day off but for Stan Kolowicz bein' sick — '

I carried the can out of the gloomy garage building, leaving the truck driver bellowing into the wall-telephone.

Back along the highway I walked, keeping to the grass plot skirting the asphalt ribbon along which the Sunday drivers zoomed.

It must have been my lucky day. The coupe was standing where I left it. There were no inquisitive motor-cycle cops lurking around it, as I feared there might be.

When I'd gassed up, I caught sight of an old hat I'd thrown on the rear seat during the Florida vacation. I jammed it on my head and stripped off my jacket. Thereafter, I drove in my shirtsleeves with the hat pulled well over my eyes. The car was still a glaring red and cream coupe and a dead give-away, but I might get past some half-asleep cop who was looking out for the hatless man in the grey sharkskin the South Bend announcer described.

I got back into the stream of traffic and kept pushing south feeling as sore as a bear in a briar patch. Time was wasting all to hell, Shelmerdine's monkeys and the girl must have been miles ahead of me and I wasn't distinguishing myself any.

A cake-brained oaf like me didn't deserve such luck. I went clear through Plymouth and out the other side, passing the bend where the wide-mouthed wench advertised toothpaste from the billboard which had a wrecked sedan wrapped around it, without even seeing a cop. Maybe they were all away at the inter-station-house poker tournament.

I didn't see any cops all the way

between Plymouth and the dirt road turn-off leading to Uffotsberg, either.

That road was a museum piece of rural Americana. I expected to see a war-party of Indians come around every bend as I jounced along it.

For a guy who had police tabs on him, however, it was better than the highway. I kept on going, bumping and bouncing and thinking of a poem by Joaquin Miller: 'Crossing the Plains.'

After a long time of bouncing past fence-rails, another road appeared, intersecting the Chisholm Trail I was following. It wasn't a first-class highway, but it was surfaced, after a fashion. Close to the intersection stood a sign-post with a single finger marked: 'Uffotsberg'. There was a weary droop to the finger as though it was tired of pointing to a place nobody ever wanted to go.

So, I went to Uffotsberg.

The trucker was right. It was the second last place God made.

The second-rate road straggled along until it became the main drag of the town. Frame houses and stores stood along either side and a wooden church, with its short spire out of plumb, stood off to one side. There was also a run-down gas station, a few shade-trees, a line of lopsided telegraph poles, three or four ancient cars parked at the kerbs, half-a-dozen people and that was Uffotsberg.

It was Sunday with a vengeance, but this town looked as if it hadn't moved with any speed since the last time the Indians attacked.

An old-timer was tilted back in a chair outside one of the frame stores. He was a type. The kind of old-timer who has lived in his small town all his life and always knows better than the fellows in Washington how the country should be run.

I pulled up at the kerb opposite him. He looked at me. I could see the words passing through his head: 'Stranger. Wonder where he's from?' I was wafted by a sudden zephyr of panic. I hoped this oldster had not heard the broadcast about the wanted driver of the red and cream coupe.

'I suppose,' I called across the cracked

sidewalk. 'if I keep on straight ahead, I'll come to Rollinsville?'

The old man regarded me with an interested stare.

'Yeah,' he said, after a while. 'Y'keep straight on.'

Then, a voice behind me said:

'Hey you! Hold it!'

I turned around and saw a paunchy figure advancing. A figure in a khaki shirt, a black tie, khaki pants and a peaked cap on a big, fat head.

This took some getting over. After riding along the broad highway in safety, I had to run into a small-town cop. I didn't know where he came from, I never passed him on the street, but there he was, a fat, officious figure.

He waddled right up to the coupe and put two fat hands on the top of the door, big pink hands. At his belt, was a holstered Army Colt, as big as a beer-can. I wondered if he could do a fast draw, like a Western marshal in the old days. I also wondered whether Al and Jungle-chest had been putting their heads together. The trucker knew I was headed for

Rollinsville and Al might have heard that broadcast for all his doziness. They could have 'phoned this hick town's police outfit.

'Your car answers the description of one the state and county police have been alerted to look out for,' said the rural gendarme. He was about forty-five, with chubby jowls and a wheezy voice. I guessed his police experience was limited to standing on the street corners of this half-horse town, nodding to the folk he grew up with. 'And you answer the description of Mike Lantry, of New York, wanted in connection with a killing in South Bend. Your car has a New York registration,' he added pridefully, just to show me he was observant.

'You, yourself, are not unlike my Uncle Otto, who was killed in a fall,' I answered coldly. 'He fell down an open manhole in Dayton, Ohio, when he was transporting a load of whisky under his belt buckle. Take your hands off my car, please, officer.'

The cop blinked at me. He kept his chubby hands on the door of the car. In the background, the old-timer was sitting bolt upright and blinking as if somebody had just broken the news of McKinley's assassination. The hick cop cleared his throat.

'What's your name?' He growled it like a hard-boiled veteran of the New York Homicide Department. Maybe he'd seen one or two movies.

'Take your hands off my car, please,' I repeated.

He took them off.

'Thank you. My name's Louis O'Callaghan. I live at Jackson's Heights, New York. I'm a teller in a bank, but I'm on vacation. My wife used to be Myrtle Hicks before I married her. She has a brother named Ed and we have a dog called Skipper. Also, I take a size fifteen collar. Now, tell me your life story.' Sometimes I got scared at my own facility for lying.

The hick cop blinked again.

'I'd like to see your driving licence, please.' He was uncertain to the extent of getting courteous, anyway.

I swivelled further around to get a good

look at him and to stare at his badge, as though absorbing the number stamped on it. I turned on a highly injured voice.

'Look, officer, I'm getting sick of this. I stop in your town to ask directions and a bumptious policeman tells me I'm wanted. I don't believe in serfdom, but I do believe in common courtesy. Your attitude is most offensive. I was just passing through this town, but now I intend to find your superior and lodge a complaint. I've noted your number.'

This shook him. Possibly the hat and the shirtsleeves, throwing me out of line with the broadcast description, had him wavering from the start. My outraged attitude probably completed the process of pulling his legs from under him.

'Okay, keep your shirt on Mr. O'Callaghan.' He'd forgotten all about the driving licence.

'I'm not a vindictive man, officer, and I realise you have your duty to do,' I continued, like a touchy dowager, 'but I really think you could show more courtesy towards a law-abiding citizen . . .'

'Okay. Okay,' said the cop. He was

flushed. Maybe he had visions of his pension taking wings.

'Okay. Okay,' I replied. 'I'll let the complaints ride this time, but this incident doesn't give me a good impression of your town.'

That touched his small-town pride. He looked very crestfallen.

'Good-bye,' I snorted. I put my foot down hard and shot away from the kerb, heading out of Uffotsberg.

Just before Main Street dwindled away at my back, I turned and saw the cop and the old-timer standing at the edge of the sidewalk, watching me go. It had been a close thing.

And none of this chasing around and pow-wowing with the rural law was getting me any nearer to Joanne Kilvert and the guys who had snatched her.

I kept tearing up the second grade road, heading for Rollinsville. The sun was shining in good earnest and time was a-wasting fast. I took a sly look at one of my shoulders, half-expecting to see sawdust there. Some of the stuffing out of my head. I'd been behaving of late like I had a hole in the nogging. Bringing big trouble home to roost with Jack and Beth Kay; getting the cops on my tail — they'd have the four-state search system all primed for me by this time — and losing Joanne to the Shelmerdine monkeys.

I had a hole in the head all right.

I should have been an insurance representative or a painter of fences.

A big slice of Indiana blurred by the coupe as I kept on gunning it along the country road, also a lot of time went by before I saw any sign of life. A clutter of distant houses and trees showed on the flat horizon, maybe two miles away.

Rollinsville, I thought.

The road took a quick bend, as though suddenly stretching the monotony out of itself, then there was a long downward sweep. Halfway down the grade, was a nearer sign of life. A form of life I didn't want to see too urgently right then.

Cops.

Four of them, standing in the roadway. Waiting for me. A big black vehicle stood a little way at their backs. The paddy-waggon.

I cut the engine down and let her purr gently down the slope, delaying contact with the spread-legged, uniformed quartette until the last minute.

'Damn that fat cop,' I snarled aloud. My voice sounded like somebody rubbing a callous on his foot with the rough edge of a matchbox. That hick patrolman back in Uffotsberg must have had second thoughts and 'phoned his brothers in handcuffs at Rollinsville. And here they were, waiting for me. Four of them. There would be no way out by fast talking this time. I could feel it in my bones.

I hadn't seen their particular line in uniforms before. Light blue pants and caps and, despite the summer heat, brown leather windcheaters with big metal badges glittering on each left breast. They weren't county police, but I was pretty sure this was county territory.

Reluctantly, like a bashful maiden entering the arms of her lover, I pulled the coupe to a halt where the reception party stood.

Now, I could see three sets of characters lettered on the rear door of the paddy-waggon: 'Rollinsville Police Dept.'

Hell. Rollinsville had its own gendarm- erie, the town must be bigger than I thought. And Rollinsville was Athelstan Shelmerdine's town.

Furthermore, I was sure this was county police territory. Any Rollinsville boundary signs I may have passed must have been well camouflaged.

A hefty cop with a sergeant's chevrons opened the *tête-à-tête*. He looked like the poor man's Marlon Brando. One of his men stood with him at the driving side of my car while the remaining pair stationed themselves at the other side.

The sergeant put two big hands with dirty fingernails on the top of the car door, right next to where I was leaning my elbow, casual-like. I didn't ask him if he would please remove them.

'Is your name Louis O'Callaghan?' the sergeant asked. So that cop in Uffotsberg had tipped them off.

'Yeah,' I said. Suddenly, I felt kind of old and my mouth began to ache where Tescachelli hit it with his gun.

'In a pig's eye it is,' said the sergeant.

He pulled his lips back, baring long teeth. The two cops at the off-side came running around the front of the car. The sergeant swung the door of the coupe open with a quick action and grabbed hold of my shoulders. One of the others gave him a hand — a couple of them, in fact.

'Like hell you're Louis O'Callaghan,' the sergeant panted. 'You're Lantry, the private eye who shot a guy in South Bend — and we want you.' They hauled me out of the car. I tried to fight back, but I hit the dirt of the road before I knew what was happening.

I had a fleeting impression of the cops grouping themselves around me, with their legs spread wide. I began to pick myself up but never got around to reaching my full height.

There was a speedy movement from the sergeant and a baton appeared in his hand. It was even bigger than a New York cop's night-stick. The sergeant's pals made the same quick movement and similar clubs appeared in their hands.

For the next few minutes, I had the

distinct impression that every cop in Indiana marched down that road and took a swipe at me with his club, with one or two guys who'd been out on pension for a while joining the clubbing-party, just by way of reliving the old days.

The last thing I remembered was looking at my shoulder to see how much sawdust they had knocked out of the hole in my head.

5

A room came into being around me, but I didn't pay much attention to it at first. I was too distracted by the armoured column that was trying to force its way out of my head.

Tanks, bashing and pounding and grinding caterpillar tracks against the inside of my skull. I lay back on whatever my aching bones had been laid out on and waited until the battle inside my head subsided. Then I opened my eyes again, slowly and with effort.

The little room crowded in on me.

A small room, a small window with bars, high on one wall; a small bunk, on which I lay. A cell.

'So, you're in jail,' I said to myself, not quite aloud.

'Yeah,' I replied. 'Wonder what the charge is.'

'Running around the landscape with a hole in your head.'

'They can't jail me for that.'

'Look around you, Mac, then reconsider that last statement.'

I shook my head and tried to think straight.

Very slowly, seeping through what the battling tanks had left of my skull, it came. As it came, it hurt, like iodine being poured into a cut.

I remembered the cops and their clubs and the paddy-waggon waiting to carry what was left of me away after they got through with their batting practice.

Taking it very easy, I sat up on the bunk, holding my head. The cops in the blue pants and leather windcheaters had put knots on it. I thought of those cops in somewhat colourful terms. I was still sure they had been poaching on county territory and I was stolen game.

The door of the cell was wide open, which surprised me. On the other side of the barred postage-stamp sized window, I could see the half-hearted darkness of a summer night.

I thought suddenly of Joanne Kilvert. I had to get out of here quick.

The floor made a couple of attempts to spring up and swipe me under the chin as I wobbled over it towards the open door. But I made it to the narrow and dingy passageway outside.

I didn't bargain for one of the blue trousered, leather jacketed club swingers being in the passageway, but he was, leaning against a dirty wall and smoking a cigarette.

For a second, he watched me stagger out of the cell with a sort of superior disgust, like an old lady on the way home from a charity meeting watching a drunk rolling out of the swing doors.

Then he grabbed me and bawled: 'Hey, chief! He's come round!'

From the far end of the passageway, a yellow-lit cloud cuckoo land which I couldn't bring into focus any too well, a voice growled: 'Bring him in here — and keep him quiet.'

The cop pushed me along the passage-way and into the yellow-lit world which turned out to be the inevitable back room of any police station. For a little while, I stood there, blinking my eyes to get used to the yellow light, issuing from under a fly-blown shade up near the ceiling. Then the cop showed me into a hard chair.

There was an old-fashioned desk at one side. A fat guy in shirtsleeves was sitting at it, talking into a telephone. He was saying: 'Yes, Mr. Shelmerdine. Yes, Mr. Shelmerdine,' time after time. I wonder if those were the only words his mother had taught him when he was a baby. I didn't like the look of the fat guy. He was all jowl and paunch and shiny bald head. There were big patches of sweat on his shirt and he was all trussed up in shoulder holster harness, like a Thanksgiving Day turkey.

The big sergeant was sitting on a chair close to a door in the far wall.

The fat guy at the desk went on saying: 'Yes, Mr. Shelmerdine.' The sight of his shoulder holster made me take a look under my jacket — which the considerate cops had apparently taken from my car and put on my back before bundling me into the paddy-waggon. The harness was still there, but no gun.

The well-known impartial observer

would probably say I sat there a long time, looking very stupid.

At the desk, the chief of police continued to say: 'Yes, Mr. Shelmerdine.' After he'd said it eight or ten times more, I got the hang of the situation. Mr. Shelmerdine was speaking to him.

This was Shelmerdine's town and these were Shelmerdine's cops.

I started to raise hell.

'You can't do this to me,' I bawled. 'You can't hold me. What's the charge? Where's my car? I want a lawyer! I'm Louis O'Callaghan, from Jackson's Heights!'

The fat guy slapped a hand over the mouthpiece of the 'phone.

'Shut him up!' he snarled. 'Give him some coffee or something.'

The two uniformed cops were within inches of me. I could smell the serge of their pants and the leather of their jackets.

'Shut up,' said the poor man's Marlon Brando. 'We know you're Lantry, the shamus from New York. We found your card in your pocket. Quit hollerin' an' stay shut up.'

I could see their clubs slapping against their thighs.

So I shut up.

'What did you have to hit him so damned hard for?' snarled the chief. 'You knocked him half screwy.' He took his hand from the mouthpiece and continued to say 'yes, Mr. Shelmerdine'.

The patrolman crossed to a perculator on a greasy table in a corner and returned with strong coffee which helped me a lot. The sergeant sat on his seat by the door, watching me while I drank it.

At the desk, the chief had changed his tune. Mr. Shelmerdine was through talking to him and the process was reversed. He was talking to Mr. Shelmerdine.

'Sure, Mr. Shelmerdine. I Understand, Mr. Shelmerdine. Not In The Police Waggon, Mr. Shelmerdine. In The Car, With No Police Uniform In Sight . . . '

You could hear the capitals. As if Mr. Shelmerdine was some kind of supreme being.

The coffee helped to take some of the screwiness out of me.

I didn't like this set-up one bit. I

had been pulled in by these Rollinsville cops who are obviously no more than dressed-up Shelmerdine hoods. I looked around quickly, on the wild hope that I might make some kind of a fight and get out of the place. No good. Too much weight against me, not to mention the cops' clubs.

Big Chief Hole-in-the-Head was in one very tight spot.

The chief of these hick-town storm troopers finished his conversation with the supreme being and clicked the 'phone down into its cradle. He swivelled about in his chair and regarded me with eyes that were almost lost in folds of fat. His large nose was touched with a very becoming shade of purple.

'Private dick,' he said. There was a deep disdain in his voice. I thought he was going to spit, but he just about managed to restrain himself.

'What's the big idea of pulling me in when I wasn't even in your jurisdiction?'

'You're anybody's game, buster. Jurisdiction don't come into it. You're wanted for shooting a guy and you've been pulled in,' he said flatly. Then he sniggered.

I sniggered. Even though I had damned little enough to snigger about.

'So you're going to turn me over to the South Bend police,' I said.

The chief sniggered again.

I knew full well these Rollinsville cops would not turn me over to the South Bend police. They were so many Shelmerdine torpedo-men and I was caught.

After a little while a car grunted to a halt outside the door close to which the sergeant sat in his tilted-back chair. Ike Tescachelli, of the neat moustache, came in with four hoods at his back, following him like small-fry shipping in the wake of a big steamer. One of them was the lean and hungry Slats. The three remaining gentlemen were new to me.

Tescachelli glowered at me. I liked his glower less than I liked the feel of his automatic slapping into my mouth.

The door was open behind the Shelmerdine mobsters and I could hear the motor of a car thrumming in the darkness outside.

'Thanks for holding him, Chief Richards,' grunted Tescachelli. 'We'll take it from here.'

'It' was me, and they weren't notably genteel about 'taking' me.

I put up a feeble sort of trouble, but didn't stand a chance with the odds against me. Somebody clapped a big hand that tasted of nicotine over my mouth and I was carted bodily out of the police station. The door in the wall of the back room gave on to a dark alley where a big saloon crouched, growling.

They bundled me into the car. Tescachelli sat beside one of the other hoods who drove while the remainder crowded into the rear compartment, holding me down to the seat. The car couldn't have seemed more crowded if the Republican party held its convention in it.

I did not get much of a chance to see the sight of Rollinsville as the saloon jerked out of the alley and went down what I took to be Main Street.

The hoods were crowding on me so intently that I only caught sight of a few lighted windows, a movie theatre with a glittering awning and one or two buildings, then we were out of town and driving through the darkness. There were trees on either side of the road and we seemed to be well and truly in the sticks.

Nobody spoke, which was just as well by me. I was still woozy and I doubted if these representatives of the Great Un-principled would have added anything to the world's store of eloquence, anyway.

The driver swerved the saloon suddenly and I had a glimpse of high gateposts flashing past, then the car purred along a driveway that seemed as long as 42nd Street and shuddered to a halt.

The strong-arms hauled me out without ceremony. Standing in the night was a mansion that looked like the sort of place people write historical romances around. It had wide steps and white pillars in the old Colonial style, but I wasn't allowed too much time to drink in the building's architectural beauty.

Tescachelli prodded me in the ribs with his gun.

'Don't make no noise,' he advised me.

'Mr. Shelmerdine don't want his wife and child wakened up.'

He prodded me up a narrow path running to the side of the house and the rest of the boys came along, just to be sociable.

Tescachelli shoved me up a short flight of steps and into a small door that was probably reserved for the servants back in the days when a dollar was a dollar.

He and his friends further persuaded me to take a short walk through what had obviously once been the exclusive domain of the serfs, then Tescachelli's gun prodded me through another door which led to the mogul's territory.

Anyone who really believes crime doesn't pay — materially, at least — should have seen that place. My guard of honour took me along a soft carpeted corridor. There was an opulent scent of beeswax polish in the air and the paintings on the walls were not cheap reproductions.

We came to a larger room and I was shoved into the presence of Athelstan Shelmerdine himself.

Only Tescachelli and Slats entered with me. The other hoods remained in the corridor. Maybe they were too much of the hoodlum class to be near Shelmerdine, too much of a reminder of the days when he himself had been pretty close to the gutter.

Shelmerdine was big. The room was big.

But I wasn't interested in either at first glance. I was interested in Joanne Kilvert, sitting on a chair in the centre of the wide sward of carpet. There was nothing dramatic about the set-up, she wasn't bound and gagged. She simply sat there, demure as a nursemaid being interviewed for a job. But she was somewhat peaked and pale. And the sniffles had developed into a heavy cold, I could tell when she said: 'Hi!' when I entered.

She was trying hard to be breezy and cocky and I admired her for it.

Shelmerdine was sitting behind a desk. It's funny the way they get a desk-complex when they hit big time gangsterdom. Mussolini had a thing about sitting behind a large desk, so had Hitler.

Shelmerdine was fat and grey and he

had a smart little moustache which made him look just like any business-man who drove to the office six mornings out of seven and played a reasonable round of golf.

There was nothing about him to suggest the old booze-running days when they settled their disputes in Chicago with sub machine-guns. He had rings under his eyes, like a fellow who worried about his stocks and bonds, his nose was kind of flat and he had a flashy mouth.

A hood, a youngster who was just learning the trade, was hovering at his back, keeping a fishy eye on Joanne. I wasn't much interested in him, but the room was something to take in.

A big french-window stood off to one side, three walls were hung with expensive looking paintings and a huge chandelier swung from the ornate ceiling. The fourth wall, backing Shelmerdine's desk, was one huge bookcase.

I eyed the titles. History. The books ran the gamut from popular stuff like Wells' *Outline of History* to works by present-day American historians like Durant and the Englishmen, Toynbee and Trevelyan.

I've heard of racketeers who opened flower-shops, owned racehorses and there were some who helped out the people they sprang from, like Al Capone, who opened soup kitchens for the Chicago poor during the depression.

With Shelmerdine, it was academic pretensions. He read history.

'You're a fool, Lantry,' he said, as Tescachelli clicked the door behind me. It wasn't a particularly hostile observation. He could have been quietly chiding me for making a business investment he thought unwise. 'You're a fool, Lantry. You stuck your nose into the wrong business when you shoved it into this one. I'm afraid I have little time for private detectives. They're fine for divorce-snooping, I suppose, but altogether too exasperating when they interfere with a man's business.'

'That's what you are — a business-man,' I observed. 'A neat line in general racketeering behind legitimate fronts — with the old-fashioned pay-off, Chicago style, when something snarls up a deal.'

Shelmerdine shuddered slightly. I guess he liked to keep the old Chicago memories thirty years at his back. Tescachelli nudged me roughly and said: 'Shaddap' in his usual tones.

Shelmerdine sniffed, like a butler suffering from injured dignity. He reached out a pair of neatly manicured hands and fondled a package that lay plumb centre on the desk. I recognised it as the package of incriminating papers Joanne had taken from his safe.

'Our Miss Jones was a very foolish young lady when she thought she could get away with these papers,' went on Shelmerdine. 'I may say I'm rather surprised at your organisation sending personable young girls on such a mission as you entrusted to Miss Jones, but your method of penetration was very neat — though it was rather opportune for you that I chose her to replace my original secretary.'

This shook me. The fact that I had been found to have a connection with the girl had made the Shelmerdine crowd think she was one of World Wide's agents.

'I've heard of your organisation, Lantry,'

went on Shelmerdine. 'I thought it was a smooth-running outfit — the crude business of your shooting Speedy Kornes and leaving him spreadeagled on a lawn in residential South Bend rather belies that impression. The radio newscasts paint quite a vivid picture of poor Speedy lying there, butchered by a private eye, and the South Bend police are hunting high and low for you. Not that Speedy was valuable to me, he wasn't — he was a dope. However, the incident is likely to bring an unwelcome focus upon me and my business, and your lady operator and yourself have been handling papers which I prefer to reserve for my own eyes. I'm afraid settlement in what you earlier termed 'Chicago style' is indicated for Miss Jones and yourself, Lantry. Shall we say a long car-ride to Lake Michigan, followed by a permanent swimming trip for you two. It will be a pity in Miss Jones' case, both my wife and child were fond of her.'

I heard Joanne give a little gasp.

I knew the type of swimming trip Shelmerdine meant. A dip in the water for two — wearing concrete boots to make sure it was for keeps.

Athelstan Shelmerdine's smooth talk snapped me out of the wooziness brought on by the clubs of his pocket police force. It was my turn to talk and I began to talk fast. He thought Joanne Kilvert was one of my operators. Let him think that.

'Listen, Shelmerdine,' I hooted. 'Do you think World Wide Investigations is a collection of dumb-clucks? You don't stand a chance of rubbing out Miss Jones and myself. World Wide is watching this place and your territory in general. You're washed up, Shelmerdine, you and all your hangers-on, from the smooth business-men in your front organisations to the cheap bums from the other side of the tracks who do your trigger-work . . . '

Tescachelli nudged me heftily.

'Shaddap,' he snorted.

I turned around on him.

'Shaddap yourself,' I told him.

And he did.

Shelmerdine was standing now, leaning his hands heavily on the big desk. Behind him the youthful mobster was looking a little agitated.

'What do you suppose we did all that time in South Bend?' I asked Shelmerdine. 'Don't bother to guess, I'll tell you. We made copies of everything in that package — typewritten copies of every document Miss Jones took from the safe. That's all we ever intended to do. Miss Jones was to return the papers as soon as we had completed the copies. That was the original plan, of course. If it had been pulled off smoothly, you would be none the wiser. Miss Jones would have returned the papers to where she found them and would have continued working with you until the copies we took caused your little empire to explode under your shoes. Things got a little snarled up, but we took those copies, and they are already on their way to the Crime Commission in Chicago. You're through, Mr. Athelstan Shelmerdine, even if you do finish off Miss Jones and I.'

Shelmerdine was white. My fast talk was working, I could tell by the way he blanched and the way the kid mobster at the rear of his chair began to jitter even more noticeably. I took a sly glance around me.

Ike Tescachelli was at my back, with his gun in his hand. Slats was standing a little way at his back, looking lean and hungry and scared. Of the three hoods, only Tescachelli was flourishing a gun. The jitters were contagious, passed on from their boss, who was obviously affected by my bluff. Only he knew what was in that package — and he knew that copies of the documents it contained, if placed in the hands of the Crime Commission, were sufficient to break him.

I thought of the nearness of Tescachelli with his gun, the distance between the french-window and myself and the position of Joanne Kilvert, seated between the window and me. I continued talking:

'Don't think this is bluff, Shelmerdine. You know those papers can ruin your whole combine.' I nodded to his pretentious books on history. 'You should know that every empire crumbles eventually. Yours started to dissolve when we made copies of those papers . . . '

I kept on talking, fast. And it was working. Shelmerdine and his hoodlums were falling for the spiel, hook, line and sinker.

While I talked, I thought of Tescachelli and his gun, wondering how fast the remaining mobsters could produce their cannon if I managed to turn on Tescachelli and whip the automatic from his hand. Then there were the other hoods who stayed outside when Tescachelli shoved me into the room, if they were still outside the door, I would have them to contend with if too much noise was made.

I kept talking, unnerving Shelmerdine. I remembered a judo move.

And risked it.

In mid-sentence, I whirled around, grabbed Tescachelli's gunhand by the wrist, using both hands. I shoved one leg diagonally across the mobster's shins and hauled on his arm with the same action.

He went hurtling forward, taken completely by surprise, hitting the expensive carpet with his face and dropping the gun. I made a dive for the weapon and yelled to Joanne: 'Run for the window!'

I had a blurred impression of Slats and the young hood moving for their guns as I grabbed Tescachelli's automatic.

Tescachelli was rolling about the floor,

holding the fine Italian nose that had contacted squarely with the floor. I came to my feet, trying to make myself into an uncoiling spring.

Slats and the youngster had their guns clear of their clothing, Shelmerdine came waddling around the desk. He was jittery, his smooth talk was gone.

'No gunplay here,' he wheezed. 'Not here. My wife and child — '

Vaguely, I wondered if his wife henpecked him. Maybe the little woman would give him hell if she found bullet-holes and spent cartridges around the place.

Shelmerdine was within grabbing distance. So I grabbed him.

I grabbed his fat neck from behind, crooking my forearm over his gizzard and yanking him backwards towards the french-window. From the corner of my eye I could see Joanne over by the window. She had moved fast and was already unfastening the clasp.

Slats and the kid mobster froze into static positions, holding their guns. My move in grabbing Shelmerdine had confused them.

I backed to the window, dragging Shelmerdine's weight with me. I put the mouth of the gun behind one of his ears.

Then I spotted the package of papers in the centre of Shelmerdine's desk. I should have grabbed that before I grabbed Shelmerdine.

I must have still been woozy, not quite out of the character of Big Chief Hole-in-the-Head.

'Run for the car on the main drive-way,' I shouted to Joanne Kilvert and I heard the clatter of her heels on the paving outside the window.

Then I gave the whole of my bluff away, proving that no copies of the original papers had been sent to the Crime Commission, by angling back over the room, prodding Shelmerdine before me, to retrieve the package.

And, cautiously, the door was being opened by the remainder of the mobsters who brought me to the mansion and who had obviously been waiting in the hall.

6

I muffed it badly.

The very fact that I was going after the package of papers on Shelmerdine's desk was proof that my story about copies of the documents being on the way to the Crime Commission was so much bluff.

I kept on pushing my hostage towards the big desk, anyway, holding the automatic close to his ear.

The mugs who came spilling into the room halted in their tracks when they saw what was going on. Tescachelli had managed to pick himself up and was standing uncertainly in the centre of the room, fingering his streaming nose. Slats and the youthful hood, like the armed monkeys who came rushing in from the passageway outside, stood motionless with guns in their hands.

'Don't try shooting, any of you,' I warned them. 'In the first place, Mr. Shelmerdine objects to anything so sordid as gunfire wakening his wife and kid; in the second, one attempt to shoot from you monkeys ends with a slug in Shelmerdine's head.'

I reached the table while the hoods stood around petrified.

At my back I felt a light summer breeze drifting in through the open french-window, reminding me that Joanne was somewhere out in the night.

Shelmerdine spotted my fast talk as so much bluff when he realised why I was shoving him back towards the desk. He started to gurgle something:

'The papers — he was ly — '

I turned off his gurgle by forcing my forearm harder against his Adam's apple.

I was faced with a problem when it came to taking the package from the centre of the desk. I had to have a free hand to do so and, holding the big-shot mobster by the neck with my left arm and my gun in my right hand, meant I had to forfeit one or the other.

So I got rid of Shelmerdine.

Crooking my knee into the small of his back, I loosed my grip about his neck and shoved him hard, in the direction of the frozen hoodlums over by the door.

I gave him all the force I could muster, and he went staggering across the room as though he had been fired from a catapault, hit the cluster of armed hoods and sprawled to the floor, panting and making a noise like a wounded duck.

I grabbed the package from the desk, turned and hared for the open french-window. There was a confused scuffle at my back, and I heard Shelmerdine wheeze something about no shooting.

But one of the hoodlums ignored his warning and fired just as I was running out of the window. I heard the slug go spanging into the ornate beading close to the drapes.

That was the signal for the remainder of the hoods to open up. Shelmerdine's taboo on shooting was thrown to the winds and, just as I was clear of the window, running out beyond the oblong of light thrown from the lighted room, a crackle of gunfire zipped into the darkness.

I was on a lawn in the darkness,

running in a mad zig-zag and trying to figure out the geography of the place to find the main drive and the car.

I came to a clump of bushes, heard a cacophany of yells at my back and ducked low as a gun barked. Still running and still crouched, I dived into the shrubbery and went crashing through a thick tangle of branches. Whoever was coming after me was close behind, but I didn't look back. I kept on beating my way through the clump of greenery, clutching the package of papers in one hand and the gun taken from Tescachelli in the other.

I came out on a path. Up ahead, a voice called: 'This way, Lantry!' A feminine voice. Joanne.

I went haring across the path in the direction of the voice. The hoods were crashing through the shrubbery behind me. After the path came a strip of lawn and, beyond that, I caught sight of the car, standing on the main drive with its motor running.

Joanne had reached the car and already had it warmed up. I could see her blanched face watching from the window.

I zig-zagged for the car, the pony express never moved faster.

Another gun blasted behind me and the slug went sailing past my ear, like a hot hornet — and too near. I figured it was time I did some shooting, so I turned as I ran and blasted a couple of shots at the hoodlums at my back, then concentrated on zig-zagging for the car.

I reached it. Joanne Kilvert was holding the off-side door open, and she put the saloon into motion as I threw myself into it. The car was in the position in which the Shelmerdine mobsters had left it when they took me into the house. It was facing the mansion, and Joanne had to put it into a sharp swerve to bring it around to face the big ornamental gateway down there at the end of that driveway as long as 42nd Street.

A fusillade of shots zipped around the saloon as she completed the circle. One of them starred the rear window.

'Give it the gun!' I yelled to the girl, as she pulled the saloon round for the straight run. Then I leaned from my window and fired two or three times at

120

the vague figures out in the darkness.

Mrs. Shelmerdine and the youngster would be well awake by this time, I figured. I wondered whether she was at that moment stalking downstairs in her dressing-robe to start henpecking Athelstan.

Joanne Kilvert was a good driver. She jockeyed the car along the length of the drive without using the lights. We made the ornamental gates. 'Head for anywhere but Rollinsville,' I told the girl, 'the cops there are Shelmerdine's puppets — and they have damned big clubs!'

She swung the vehicle off in the opposite direction to that which led to Rollinsville.

'Where will this road take us?' I asked.

'I don't know, I never had a lot of time to study the geography of these parts.'

She spoke thickly. The cold she had caught as a result of the soaking rain of the previous day was a heavy one, and she was still clad in only the light summer dress.

She was bearing up well, but, with that cold, she must have been feeling even worse than me — and I felt like something somebody had chewed and spat out. I was hungry for one thing, the last time I ate was at the Kay's house where we breakfasted. I guessed Athelstan Shelmerdine's hospitality would not run to providing the girl with a meal while she was his unwilling houseguest.

There was a panicky confusion racing around in my head. I had the package of incriminating papers in my pocket, and I had to get them to the Crime Commission somehow. At the same time, I was wanted in connection with the shooting at South Bend. The four-State search system would be in action. I was hot stuff, and I had a pocketful of hot stuff that had to be placed before the Commission somehow, then there was the girl.

Shelmerdine thought she and I knew too much about his activities, and his way of dampening our ardour would be concrete weights for two and a couple of splashes in some quiet corner of Lake Michigan when the moon was hiding behind a cloud.

'Boy,' I thought, 'were two people ever in such a mess?'

Joanne kept driving for a while. The road was not too good, but we could not risk using the headlamps. There was a silence behind us that was far too ominous for my peace of mind.

I took over the wheel, and we burned up the road for several miles without seeing another vehicle, a person or a lighted window. Joanne sat huddled on the seat beside me, looking a little scared, but nothing like the jittery youngster I picked up in the rainstorm.

I wondered how things were with Jack and Beth Kay in South Bend. If all had gone smoothly Jack would have contacted Walt Toland in Chicago by that time, and there should soon be some action from my Chicago branch office. Driving blind through the night, along that rutted road, I tried to figure out a plan of action.

Chicago was the obvious place to make for with that red hot package, but we would have to reach the Windy City by making a detour around South Bend. Anywhere in the mid-West was hot for me since that shooting at Jack Kay's house, but South Bend was the storm-centre.

In the gloom I saw a narrow dirt road branching off the one on which I was driving. As I passed it, I realised how it was almost hidden by high, wild hedges on either side. An idea struck me, and I jerked the saloon into reverse.

'What are you doing?' asked Joan Kilvert, alarmed.

'Remember the time we turned up that dirt road when Shelmerdine's hoodlums were after us yesterday?'

She nodded.

'Well, we're working the same gimmick, but with variations.'

I pulled the saloon into the opening of the side-road. It was little more than a cart-track, and the car jounced heavily over ruts and rocks. I pulled it sharply across to the overhanging greenery fringing the road and braked with the windows hard against the shrubbery.

'Okay, we'll wait here for a little while,' I told Joanne. 'Keep your eyes glued on that rear window, and I predict you'll see some activity.'

About ten minutes ticked by. We sat in the darkness, twisted about in our seats, watching the road we had left.

Powerful headlights streamed along it suddenly as the roar of engines sounded from the direction of Shelmerdine's little palace.

Two cars, heavy shadows with white lights raying from them, went rocketing by, disappeared into the darkness, and the combined tune of their powerful motors died away.

'The dogs are out, girlie,' I grunted. 'It's my guess Shelmerdine has sent his search parties to every point of the compass. This territory is going to be plenty hot for two people whose names I need not mention. How many cars are there around Shelmerdine's place?'

'Five or six, I guess,' Joanne replied. 'That's counting this one.'

'Which means there are at least two more scouting around some other area. Then, there are a bundle of cops in Rollinsville who belong to Shelmerdine. We'll have to watch out for those boys.'

'What's our next move?' she asked.

'To get to Chicago pronto, like a couple of mice getting out of a closet full of cats.

125

I told Jack Kay to call Walt Toland, head of my Chicago agency, and tell him what had happened, so the chances are we'll have some World Wide operators around here in a few hours. I might be able to contact them in some way, but our best hope is to keep moving Chicago-wards.'

We sat in the car for about twenty minutes more. There was no sign of life on the road ahead of us, and the land was shrouded in silent darkness. I decided to risk moving from the hiding-place, started up the motor and sent the saloon nosing slowly forwards, to bring it into a turn that set its face towards the road we had left earlier.

I still drove without lights. Clear of the rutted minor road, I headed in the direction we had originally taken once more. I had a secret dread of encountering the two cars that Shelmerdine had sent in that direction, returning. I guess Joanne had the same fear by the way she peered through the windshield and into the darkness ahead, but she kept her fear well hidden.

At length, we came to another small

road, branching off to the left.

I turned the car into it.

'I'm going to try angling around to the north on a wide detour,' I told the girl. 'We'll keep to the smaller roads and try to make Chicago, avoiding the towns around here and South Bend.'

She didn't reply. I glanced at the slight figure on the seat beside me and realised she was asleep.

I thought of the strain she had been through during the previous few hours and did not disturb her. She was curled up in the seat breathing gently, like a tired child. I remembered the way she stood under that tree when we hid from the Shelmerdine mugs in the rain of the previous night. Anybody's kid sister, but so darned full of guts!

She was getting at me through the chinks in my armour again, and I knew that the trickiest chore Mike Lantry ever faced was right before him — to get that girl out of Athelstan Shelmerdine's territory alive and with the package of papers for the Crime Commission's attention.

I drove steadily, still without lights, along that bumpy side-road. As I drove, I thought of the mess I had put myself into, with every cop for miles looking for my scalp. I thought of the dirty piece of underworld I had virtually dragged out of the gutter and into the home of the Kays. I thought of Lucy waiting in New York to meet Joanne at the railroad station. I thought of Walt Toland and the boys at Chicago who, if Jack had put my message through, would come snooping around the vicinity of Shelmerdine's house, but we couldn't wait that long.

Dawn began to split the sky and gradually flushed upwards.

Joanne was still sleeping.

Against the rosy sweep of the dawning day, I saw the barns of a farm in the distance and drove towards them almost unconsciously. At the back of my mind floated the notion that there might be a telephone at the farm, and I could call Toland in Chicago with news of my position.

Then a bolder thought struck me. The farm was isolated, well off the beaten track; it might be possible for us to buy a meal there if we carried out a little play-acting.

I jockeyed the saloon along the country road until we reached the point where the yard of the farm opened on to it.

There was nothing special about the place. A clutter of high barns and smaller buildings ringed the yard, which was littered with a scatter of milk cans and crates. A depression vintage Ford truck stood in the centre of the yard, half-loaded with hay bales and a horse who looked as old as Methuselah's cat regarded us from over the half-door of a rickety stable.

I gave Joanne a nudge, and she rose to wakefulness, looking around her in alarm. I braked the car close to the farm-yard gate.

'I'm going to try for a meal here,' I said. 'We'll have to pretend we're married. We're heading for South Bend in a roundabout way, and we've come up from Kokomo. Call me Al, or something, just in case these farm folk have heard any police broadcasts. Okay?'

'Okay,' she agreed.

I straightened my tie and tried to make my suit look a little less tired. There was a weight in either pocket of my jacket. The gun in one and the package of papers in the other.

Joanne rubbed the sleep from her eyes, straightened rebel strands of hair with her slender fingers and smoothed the wrinkles out of her dress.

'If only I had a compact,' she lamented, gazing at herself in the driving mirror.

'At a time like this,' I snorted, 'please don't trouble about trivialities.'

'Trivialities,' she said, shocked, as if powder compacts were the most important things in the world. It came out 'triviadities' because of her cold in the head and I grinned.

'Women! C'mon, let's take the stage.'

We walked across the yard. The farmhouse was a white frame structure standing off to one side. We mounted four plank steps giving on to a porch which had a rocking-chair standing on it and roses climbing prettily around its rails. Knowing the way farming folk live, I guessed it was not too early to find some sign of life around the house, so I tapped politely at the white-painted door.

There was a shuffling of feet on the other side of the door, and it swung open slowly.

Standing there was an old man who looked like the dear old dad of the heroine in a TV soap-opera. He wore faded blue coveralls, what hair he had was snow white, and he had a pair of steel-rimmed glasses balanced on the tip of a button of a nose. He regarded us with mild blue eyes, faded to about the same shade as his coveralls.

I turned on the charm of a nice guy in a TV soap-opera, just to match his part. Joanne stood demurely beside me.

'Excuse me, sir, I wonder whether my wife and I might buy some breakfast from you. We're heading for South Bend, and we got a little way off the beaten track.'

The old man beamed.

'Why, sure,' he said. Then he turned on his heel and bellowed: 'Hey, ma, it's two people wanting to know if we can fix 'em breakfast.'

From deep in the soul of the house a woman's voice said: 'Yes, bring 'em in.'

The farmer ushered us into a neat room. A large table stood in the centre, and the indications were that breakfast was just over.

A buxom woman issued from a doorway across the room and regarded Joanne and myself for a moment, then re-entered her sanctum. The farmer nodded to a couple of ladder-backed chairs, and we seated ourselves. The old-timer led off with some small talk about the weather, then asked where we came from.

'Kokomo,' I told him.

He nodded and said he'd been there a couple of times.

The woman entered again. This time she was carrying food. Eggs, ham, cereal, bread, biscuits and coffee. I didn't know how she contrived to rustle up breakfast as fast as that at such short notice, but it smelled good, and I wasn't going to ask any questions.

We ate.

The farmer's wife seated herself in one

of the ladder-backed chairs and watched us. She was a stout woman in a black dress and white apron. In spite of her buxom build, there was a certain prudishness about her. She looked at Joanne often.

She sniffed a couple of times, too.

'Do you have a telephone here?' I asked the farmer. 'I'd like to make a call as soon as possible.'

He nodded to a small door which I hadn't noticed before.

'Right in there. It's kinda old-fashioned, but it works.'

His wife sniffed again. I began to wonder if one of us smelled.

When the meal was finished I crossed the room in which the telephone was. It was an old type of wall phone on which a handle had to be whirled furiously around before you got into touch with the exchange. The phone was close to the door, and I stood there, whirling the handle like a Las Vegas gambler trying to coax the jackpot out of a slot machine. I could see the larger room; Joanne's back, as she was seated at the table, the buxom and prudish farm woman and the farmer, who was fiddling with the knobs of a radio of about the same vintage as his truck out in the yard.

The ear-piece of the phone crackled unrewardingly. Then I heard a voice, distant and ghostly, gabbling away somewhere in another world.

The farmer found an early morning station on the radio dial, and a newsreader came in with a monologue on world events.

The ear-piece went on crackling, and the ghost voice continued to gabble unintelligibly beyond the crackling.

'It's a party line,' drawled the farmer, who was standing by the radio, tamping shag into a corn-cob pipe. 'Maybe you'll have trouble getting through.'

'He will have trouble getting through,' confirmed his wife, 'that Mrs. Kunitz will be on — even at this time of day. She's always on.'

She sniffed again and cast another glance at Joanne. I stood there, leaning against the jamb of the door with the ear-piece held to my ear. I noticed that the farm woman's glance was directed at Joanne's hands, and the cause of her concern hit me. She doubted we were married because the girl had no wedding ring.

I snorted and listened to the buzzing and the ghost voice. Then I started in to revolve the handle again. Getting through to Chicago on that antiquated instrument seemed about as likely as getting through to Mars.

In the next room the radio newsreader finished his recital of the world's ills and came in with a flash that caused a chill knife to slide into me.

He said:

'A concentrated search is going on throughout Indiana for Mike Lantry, head of World Wide Investigations, the New York detective agency. Lantry is wanted for questioning in connection with the shooting of Paul 'Speedy' Kornes at the South Bend home of Jack Kay, at noon yesterday. Word has been received from Uffotsberg that Lantry passed through that town yesterday, headed towards Rollinsville. Rollinsville *police report that he was not seen in that vicinity . . .* '

That was cute, I thought. If the Rollinsville police, those leather-jacketed Shelmerdine puppets, did not sight me, I wondered who the guy they clubbed on that country road was. The radio continued:

' . . . *considerable mystery surrounds the South Bend shooting. The dead man served a term in Illinois State Penitentiary some years ago and is known to have been no paragon of citizenship. Kay, at whose home the shooting occurred, is described as an exemplary citizen. He told police that Lantry, an old war-time companion, called at his home the previous night with a young woman . . .* '

Standing there, with the crackling, ghost-gabbling ear-piece to my ear, I allowed myself a slight smile as the radio voice went on to reveal that Jack had told the South Bend cops only what I had wanted him to tell them.

In the next room, Joanne was sitting stiffly at the table. The farm woman was still eyeing the girl's hands slyly and disapprovingly. The farmer was building up power on his corn-cob, wreaths of blue smoke drifted around his white head.

The radio went on to give the inevitable description of me. It was all there, the scar on my face, the notch on my ear, the colour of my hair and suit.

I saw the old man's back stiffen and his wife tore her attention away from Joanne's ringless fingers and darted a quick glance in my direction.

Slowly, I placed the ancient ear-piece on the hook on the wall set. It was hopeless to continue trying to call Walt Toland on that relic. Anyway, it didn't seem to matter any more.

I didn't think the farmer could move that fast. He didn't look the part, anyway.

If anyone had told me that nice old guy could open the drawer in the table on which the radio stood, dip his hand into it and bring out a fistful of Army Colt as fast as that, I would have laughed.

Until I saw him do it.

7

I looked into the mouth of the old-timer's Army Colt and felt like a kid who had been surprised while stealing apples.

Joanne gave a little squeak and stood up from her seat at the table; the farmer's wife clucked like an alarmed hen and also stood up. She glowered at me and I glowered back.

The farmer stood quite still with the revolver levelled at me. His corn-cob was in his mouth and the mild blue eyes had become remarkably hard. The hand holding the gun didn't quaver one little bit.

'Better not move, young man,' he said. He spoke with that odd distortion of words, the way a man does when he holds a pipe clamped hard between his teeth. 'I know you're the fellow the man on the radio just spoke about. Don't think I'm fooling with this gun — I can use it if I have to.'

He ceased to be a nice old guy out of a soap opera. There was a hardness and a determination about him that told me he meant what he was saying. I figured I'd best attempt an appeal to reason.

Looking into that Army Colt, I felt like I wanted a good night's sleep.

'You deserve praise for your public spirit, Dad,' I told him, 'but there's no need for waving firearms. Suppose you put that thing away and make the whole bunch of us feel more comfortable.'

'And let you kill my wife and I the way you killed that man in South Bend? You two people stand right where you are. My hired man will show up in a few minutes and we'll hand you over to the police.'

'Now look, mister, that shooting in South Bend will be cleared up just as soon as I get in touch with the right authorities. That's what I was trying to do with that old 'phone of yours — get in touch with friends of mine. I'm on the side of law and order, Dad, an investigator — savvy?'

It was useless. The old man went right on giving me the fish-eye.

'I know your kind. A private detective. Divorces and all them kind of sordid things. Your kind are no-account, I don't wonder you get into trouble.'

The Colt still remained on me without a waver.

I got to wishing I was an insurance salesman or a fence-painter once more.

Joanne was darting alarmed glances at me and then at the farmer. The farmer's wife just stood there glaring at Joanne. I guess she was still disgusted about her lack of a wedding-ring.

I had another try.

'You're taking the wrong line, Dad — '

'Shut up!' the old man snapped. He couldn't have put more venom into it if he'd been some kin to Ike Tescachelli. 'Emmaline, call up the police.'

His wife started for the doorway in which I stood. I took a pace backwards so I was close to the telephone again.

'That Mrs. Kunitz will probably be on the line yet,' I said.

The farmer's wife came on.

'Get away from the 'phone,' said the old man.

I reached out my hand, keeping my eyes on the gun in the farmer's hand and feeling for the ear-piece on its hook on the side of the wall-box. I found it, gripped it and yanked hard, snapping it from its wire.

The farmer's wife stopped in her tracks.

'I'm sorry,' I said, 'but I can't have you calling the police, at least, not the kind of police you have in these parts.'

The farmer's hand wavered just a little. My putting the telephone out of commission that way put him on the thin edge of panic for a minute. I wondered how soon the hired man would show up and what kind of individual he would be.

Out in the yard, just visible through a segment of window, was the ancient Ford truck. I could see the old horse, still viewing the world of men over the top of the stable door. The nose of the saloon was visible, projecting from one side of the gateway. It was standing out there on the dirt-road in full view for any of the Shelmerdine crowd to see if they came this way.

There was no sign of any hired man.

And the minutes were ticking by.

The farmer, his wife and Joanne stood quite still, all three of them watching me. I tried a third attempt at reason.

'You wouldn't dare use that old hog-leg,' I said to the farmer. 'I suggest you put it away and we talk reasonably.'

He straightened his shoulders.

'I'll use it if I have to.'

I measured up the distance between the old-timer and myself. Just a few yards of clear, carpet-covered floor. Behind the farmer was the table on which the radio stood. The radio was now churning out a breakfast-time commercial, but nobody was interested.

I'd have to make sure the oldster didn't crack his head on the table if I made a football tackle for his legs. Maybe I could do it; maybe I couldn't. But I had to break this deadlock.

So I dived.

And grabbed his legs.

The farmer's wife screamed.

I pulled the old man down.

The Colt went off and put a slug in the ceiling.

The farmer's wife squawked. Joanne screamed.

I rolled on top of the gasping oldster.

I gripped the gun and wrenched it.

It came out of his hand.

Then I stood up, flipped out the cylinder and shoved the cartridges out on to the floor, put the empty Colt on the table beside the jabbering radio and helped the old man up.

'I'm sorry, but you wouldn't listen to reason,' I told him. I seated him in a chair and turned off the radio. Joanne and the farm woman stood their ground, still alarmed by the gunshot.

A little plume of acrid gunsmoke drifted flatly across the room.

'Go get him a glass of water, Joanne,' I said.

The girl went into the kitchen and returned with a tumbler of water, the old man panted and drank it.

His spouse was looking at me with two very wide eyes.

'What're you going to do to us?' she wanted to know.

'Nothing,' I told her, 'except talk some

143

sense into you. It's true that I'm the man the police are looking for because of that shooting in South Bend. Their radio flashes make me sound like a wanton killer, but that isn't so. I'll pay you for the breakfast. Just forget you saw us, huh?'

I fished in my pocket and found my wallet. Surprisingly enough, those leather-jacketed hoodlums of the Rollinsville police force left my money intact when they frisked me after taking me prisoner. I put enough to pay for four breakfasts down on the table.

Someone was whistling out in the yard. The hired man.

I turned around to look out of the window and saw him, a gangling youth with plenty of the yokel about him and little to be scared of. His heavy boots came thumping up the porch steps, he opened the house door and came in.

He stopped in his tracks, eyes flying to the Colt on the table and bugging out.

'Hey, what goes on, Mr. Whitley?' he asked.

'Nothing,' I said quickly. 'Mr. and Mrs. Whitley were good enough to provide us with some breakfast, we're passing through.'

'Oh,' said the youth. 'What for is the gun on the table?'

'I was looking at it. I know a lot about guns. They're my hobby,' I informed him.

He looked at me. I looked at him.

'Oh,' he said. The explanation seemed to satisfy him. He changed the subject. 'There's a lot of police around the top end of the road in cars. Rollinsville police. I didn't know they was supposed to come over this way.'

'Rollinsville police!' I echoed. I remembered that stolen saloon, standing outside the gate of the farmyard as a dead give away for anyone who came snooping around.

'Mr. Whitley, I'll make a bargain with you,' I told the farmer. 'I'll buy that old truck of yours, but I can't pay you right now. I'll send you a cheque just as soon as I get out of this fix, you'll have to trust me. Shall we say seven hundred dollars?'

'For that old ruin?' gurgled the farmer from his chair. 'It ain't worth — '

'Seven hundred it is, then,' I said, then

I raised the bid. 'Make it a thousand for the load of hay and a set of farmer's coveralls and an old hat.'

The old man goggled. So did his wife and the hired hand.

Whitley nodded. It was an effort for him to do so.

'What goes on?' asked the youth again.

'Nothing for you to worry about,' I told him. 'Where can a man hide a saloon in these parts — I mean dump it good so nobody would ever find it?'

'He could drive it into the old pond in the pasture up the road a small piece,' drawled the hired hand.

'How do I get to it?'

'First gate in the fence up the dirt road to the left,' the youth informed me.

I told Joanne to stay in the house and went out the door, down the steps of the porch and across the yard to where the saloon was parked. Cautiously, I looked out of the yard gate. There was no sign of activity along the road. I jumped into the saloon, started it up and took it off to the left of the road.

The gate in the white-painted fence

was only a matter of yards along the road. I climbed out of the car, opened it, then drove the saloon into the fallow field on the other side of the gate.

Before climbing back behind the wheel, I glanced along the road in both directions. Nothing in sight but a couple of crows walking along the dirt-road. Maybe their wings were tired.

I drove the car into the field, saw the pond shining in the sun with a cluster of trees around it, and headed for it.

At the edge of the water, I braked.

The pond was wide and covered with a green scum. I cut the engine, released the brakes and climbed out. At the back of the car, I began to shove with my shoulder. The vehicle began to roll, slithered over the edge and descended into the pond with a mighty, far-flung splash.

I watched it settle under the scum slowly, then made my way back to the house.

There was still no sign of life on the dirt road. Even the crows were gone.

Back in the farmhouse, I found that

Whitley had rooted out a set of old coveralls and a battered, wide-brimmed hat. Maybe it was the fact that I hadn't harmed him after pulling the gun from him, maybe it was the generous payment for the meal Joanne and I had been provided with and maybe it was the promise of the thousand dollars, but something made the farmer and his spouse treat us in a more friendly fashion.

'What goes on?' the hired man was still asking.

'These coveralls go on, son,' I answered. 'The young lady and I go off in that old heap in the yard and you don't know anything about us. Compree?'

The youth blinked.

'I'll see he doesn't know anything about it,' promised the farmer. That cheque for a thousand must have been floating before his eyes like a rosy dream.

'Good,' I said, then I pulled off my jacket, took off my tie and pulled on the coveralls. I slapped the farmer's hat on my head. My light tan Oxfords didn't go so well with the rustic get-up, but I figured on doing plenty of riding in the

148

old truck, so no one would see my feet.

'Okay,' I said to Joanne, 'let's take a hay-ride.'

She joined me and we went out the door, across the yard towards the parked truck. I looked like someone on his way to a New Year's Eve carnival, I guess. Joanne eyed me with humour reflected in her face.

'What happens to me?' she asked. 'I'm hardly dressed as a farmer's girl.'

'You go out of sight, until we are free of Shelmerdine's territory, at least,' I told her. 'I'm sorry, but you'll have to ride under the hay-bales.'

'You know best,' she shrugged.

'The Shelmerdine crowd are looking out for a man and a girl in a saloon. They'll pay very little attention to a single farmer in a beat-up old truck like this,' I explained as I bundled her on to the rear of the truck. She settled down on one of the bales and I shaped the remainder around her so she was completely hidden.

Starting up the old truck was a groan-and-sweat chore. The motor rattled into life with a noise like an earthquake hitting a junk-yard.

I climbed up behind the wheel and took the relic off along the dirt road. The green scenery rolled slowly past as I kept the nose of the truck pointed north.

More than anything else, I wanted a good night's sleep. The pounding those Rollinsville cops handed me left me tender around the head, so tender, in fact, that I had left that old Army Colt and ammunition on the table in the Whitleys' farmhouse. With one hand on the wheel, I transferred the package of papers to the pocket of the coveralls from the pocket of the jacket on the seat beside me. Also, I took the automatic from the jacket pocket.

I flipped open the magazine of the gun. The clip was half-spent and I had no more ammunition since the Rollinsville police relieved me of my spare clip of cartridges as well as my own gun.

The shoulder holster was still strapped across my chest and I pushed the weapon into it. If only I had taken the Colt and its ammunition into the bargain I made with Whitley!

I steered the truck around a gentle turn and saw the road ribboning away for some yards, then it was crossed by an interesting road.

At the crossing stood a lone figure, leaning against a motor-cycle. Even at that distance, I could see the determination on his face as he stood spread-legged in the road watching the truck approach.

He wore a peak cap, a leather jacket with a big badge and blue riding-pants with a wide yellow stripe.

A Rollinsville patrolman.

There was nothing for it but to brazen it out.

As I jockeyed the truck nearer to the cop, I saw that his face was new. He was not one of those who had been in on the clubbing party the previous day. Without making the move too obvious, I pulled the wide-brimmed hat over my eyes and braked close to the cop.

Under the hood, the engine clattered and clanged like half a dozen tin-cans being kicked along a deserted alley.

'What's the matter?' I hailed, turning on my best hick accent.

The policeman was a sharp featured individual. He looked at me like a professor scrutinising a specimen of something or other. I remembered the precise descriptions of me that had been broadcast, detailing the scar and the notch in my ear.

I felt distinctly uneasy.

'Ain't that old man Whitley's heap?' asked the cop, nodding to the truck.

I leaned from the cab window, keeping my head artfully low and my face turned so he couldn't see the scar.

'Yeah,' I told him over the din of the motor.

An amused quirk came to the corners of the policeman's mouth.

'Beats me how he keeps that wreck in working order,' he opined.

'Yeah,' I said. 'It's been dead for some years, I guess, but it's reluctant to lie down.'

The cop grinned again. He looked as though he might be a friendly guy — if he wasn't decked up in the uniform of Shelmerdine's partisan police force, complete with revolver and the inevitable

table-leg-sized club.

'You're new around here, huh?' he asked, looking at me closely. 'Don't recollect seeing you before.'

'I'm Whitley's new hired man,' I lied, 'workin' for him only a few days.'

The motor of the old rattle-trap went on chugging under the quivering bonnet. The cop went right on looking at me.

I took a sly look at the cross-roads. There was a marker pointing in the direction we had come with the legend: 'Rollinsville' and another pointing north. It said: 'Stokestown and State Highway'. A third arm pointed off along the intersecting road, marked 'Uffotsberg'.

My dopy brain began to tick over. I wanted to keep clear of both Uffotsberg and Rollinsville. The state highway, which I could reach by way of the road straight ahead, was the one leading to South Bend and on to Chicago. I was in no hurry to go to South Bend, either, but I might fool the cops in my present get-up and in the old truck.

Meanwhile, I had to get away from this too friendly patrolman.

153

'What brings Rollinsville police over this far?' I asked innocently.

The motor-cycle cop's eyes widened.

'Ain't you heard? Every cop for miles is on the look-out for a guy who murdered a fellow in South Bend. The same guy is supposed to have robbed the Shelmerdine mansion last night.'

I gave a meaningless grunt. I figured that maybe the Rollinsville police department was not entirely under the rule of the Shelmerdine combine. The chief and the senior officers would be pawns of Shelmerdine's political grafting, but there would be a number of square officers. So the story the up-and-up officers had been told was that I had robbed the Shelmerdine home!

I simulated surprise.

'Well, what d'you know!' I exclaimed. 'Nobody ever tells me anything.'

'He's some fool of a private detective playing at being a cop,' the patrolman told me. 'We'll get him sooner or later.'

'Yeah,' I said. I tuned up the motor, indicating that I wanted to be on my way. The cop removed his foot from where he had placed it on the running-board and waved his hand in a cordial farewell.

'So long,' said he.

'So long,' said I.

The truck clattered slowly across the intersecting road. the cop stood at the crossroads watching it go, I could see him in the driving mirror.

I breathed a sigh of relief when I was over the crossroads and hoped the girl was still hidden by the bales of hay.

I kept the truck headed at a steady roll in the direction of Stokestown and the state highway, went about three hundred yards from the crossroads, then trouble caught up with me.

The engine blinked out.

With a shuddering growl, the museum piece came to a stop. I swore under my breath, climbed down from the cab, went around the front and opened the hood.

There was a roar from the direction of the crossroads, I looked along the road and saw the friendly cop coming along on his motor-cycle.

'What's happening?' asked Joanne's voice from the midst of the hay bales.

'Quiet,' I warned her. 'The engine's acting up and it looks like that cop is coming to offer us some help.'

I was tinkering under the hood when he pulled up beside the old Ford. He put one foot to the ground and sat the purring motor-cycle.

'Anything drastic?' he asked.

I had just located the fault, a disconnected lead, probably brought about by the excessive vibration, and was in the act of refastening it. Turning my face about, I looked at the patrolman from under the raised hood.

I was just in time to see his eyes light on my Oxfords, visible under the legs of the old coveralls. Then, I realised that, from this angle, he could see the scar on the side of my face.

His eyes bugged slightly. He swung his leg over the motor-cycle, left the machine resting on its stand, and advanced on me. His face was set into hard lines, and he was going after the revolver at his belt.

'Wait a minute, mister,' he began in a voice like hailstones on a tin roof. I didn't wait a fraction of a minute.

The jig was up, that was obvious, so I came out from under the hood of the old Ford fast, and I came out swinging.

I handed the cop a hard crack across the jaw, which stopped him from going through with drawing his gun. He staggered back towards his purring machine, half sagging at the knees. I went right after him and swung out another fistful of knuckles, taking him square on the point of the chin.

He folded and hit the roadway with a slight groan.

It was a pity, he was a nice, helpful guy, probably one of the best on that lousy Rollinsville force, but he had spotted me, and I couldn't risk being pulled in.

The cop lay there, sprawled out beside his still buzzing machine, quite still on the ground. One of the hay bales stirred on the rear of the truck, and Joanne's face peered out of an aperture between two of the bundles.

'What's happened?' she wanted to know.

'I've slugged the cop, knocked him cold. He spotted me, my shoes gave me away first, then he saw the scar on my face.'

'What're you going to do?'

'Get out of here quickly and make sure he takes a long time in getting word of our movements back to his friends.'

I dragged the unconscious cop across the deserted road and laid him out on the grass verge. The big Colt in his holster looked like a better investment against my running into any shooting than the automatic with the half-spent clip I already carried, so I took it and pushed it into the pocket of the coveralls.

Next, I crossed to the motor-cycle, cut its motor, pulled out its spark-plugs and hurled them far into the field. That would keep him from reaching his buddies in a hurry.

Over where he lay in the grass tract running alongside the road, the cop groaned.

'Too bad it had to happen to a nice guy like you, Clancy,' I said to the half-conscious form. 'I guess Chief Richards will fire you for this, but you'd be better off digging ditches than working on that stinking Rollinsville force.'

The cop grunted again and made a feeble movement.

I climbed into the cab of the Ford again after swinging the crank. My temporary repair job on the broken wiring worked. With Joanne Kilvert still hidden in the bales of hay, I piloted the truck in the direction of Stokestown and the state highway.

The weight of the purloined Colt in my coveralls was very comforting.

8

Stokestown.

Not much of a place, but we made it without running into further trouble.

It was another single-street town with brick stores, frame houses and a little square, shaded by sycamore trees, where the oldsters of the town sat on green-painted benches. It was the sort of place that only came alive on the fourth of July.

The old Ford truck rattled its way along the street and I didn't see one cop. Uppermost in my mind, was the need to contact the Chicago office of World Investigations. The attempt on that ancient 'phone at the Whitley farmhouse had been hopeless, but I figured there was a chance that I would find a telephone somewhere in this sleepy little burg.

The few folk on the street paid little attention on the old truck with its load of hay bales, I guessed beaten-up old vehicles, belonging to small farmers, were nothing unusual out in this rural retreat.

I saw an attractive sign swinging outside a neat brick building: 'The Busy Bee Cafe'. It brought tempting visions of hot coffee and, most of all, a telephone. There was an alley to one side of the eating-house, wide enough to take the truck. I decided to risk a call at the cafe, swung the truck into reverse and backed down the alley. I braked.

The alley was deserted and quiet. Out round the back of the truck, I told Joanne we were taking a rest and helped her out of her hiding place.

She came down off the back of the truck gratefully, brushing wisps of hay from her dress and hair.

We walked cautiously around to the main street and into the cafe.

There was a counter along one side and a half-asleep youth in a white coat was draped across it. There were half a dozen tables with checkered tablecloths and a small telephone booth was squeezed into one corner.

The youth stirred leisurely into consciousness.

'Coffee?' he asked.

'Coffee?' I asked Joanne.

'Coffee,' she agreed.

'Coffee,' I ordered.

The youth yawned and slowly got around to rustling up two cups of coffee. I crossed to the telephone booth while he was about it.

I had just enough nickels for the long-distance call to Chicago. The instrument went through the usual preliminary buzzings and clickings while I stood impatiently staring out of the window of the booth, across the cafe and out of the window fronting the street.

The Chicago agency answered.

'Lantry,' I announced. 'Is that Walt?'

A splutter of surprise came from the other end. 'No, this is O'Toole. Walt and four of the boys are running around some part of Indiana looking for you. Your friend in South Bend called and told us where you went. What's been happening? Where are you?'

'Take it easy, O'Toole,' I said. 'Let me do the talking. I'm in a place called Stokestown, a one-horse burg off the state

162

highway. Can you get into radio contact with Walt Toland and his boys?'

'Yes.'

'Then tell him I'm in Stokestown with the girl and the papers. The police are on my tail for shooting a hoodlum in South Bend and the Shelmerdine bunch are after me, too. Tell Walt I'm heading for Chicago in an old Ford truck loaded with hay. I don't know how long this will last, though, I had to slug a cop and when he gets to squawking about what happened to him, I expect to have plenty of trouble on my hands.'

'You're in Stokestown, heading for Chicago in a hay-truck, Ford,' checked O'Toole.

'Yeah,' I said, 'and tell Toland and his boys to come running in this direction. Shelmerdine threatened to dip the girl and myself into Lake Michigan — with concrete boots. We gave him the slip, but it can't happen a second time. Oh, and ring Lucy in New York. Tell her she can quit waiting for that train now, the Kilvert girl isn't coming.'

'Check,' said O'Toole.

There was a concentrated clicking and buzzing. My time was up and I'd had my money's worth.

I joined Joanne back at the counter. The youth in the white coat was well on the way to becoming half asleep again.

The girl clutched my arm urgently.

'Mike, while you were in the call box, I saw a Cadillac go past the window. It looked like the one belonging to Tescachelli, the one they took me away from South Bend in.'

I felt a cold stab at that and took a sip of coffee.

'Maybe you were mistaken. There are a lot of cars of that type around.'

Her eyes were on the window of the cafe; outside, Stokestown inhabitants moved slowly about their main street. I drank my coffee slowly, watching passing pedestrians and cars.

I began to wonder whether the cop I slugged had succeeded in contacting his pals; then again, maybe the girl had been mistaken about the Cadillac being Tescachelli's.

But she wasn't.

The big Cadillac came nosing into view, moving slowly along like a tired bug. I had a brief glimpse of Ike Tescachelli at the wheel.

Instantly, I realised that the car had travelled past the cafe, its occupants had caught sight of the old truck parked in the alley, turned and travelled back.

It halted close to the kerb on the opposite side of the street. I grabbed Joanne and moved her quickly towards a section of blank wall at one side of the window.

'Do you think they saw us?' she asked, alarmed.

'I don't know, but they saw the truck for sure and they've pulled up across the street.'

I felt for the comforting weight of the Colt I had removed from the cop's holster, and my hand came into contact with the package of papers taken from Shelmerdine's safe.

The youth in the white coat snapped himself into wakefulness, he regarded us quizzically as we pressed ourselves against the wall, out of view from the street.

'You got a back way out of here?' I asked him.

He jerked his head towards a small door at the rear of the counter.

'Only that way, through the kitchen and into the alley.'

'Look,' I said, 'would you be good enough to step over to the window and take a look out on the street. Tell us if there's a big Cadillac parked right across from here and whether the guys in it show any signs of coming across here?'

He gave me another quizzical look.

'Private dicks,' I said, nodding in the general direction of the street, 'the lowest form of life in the universe. You know how it is, her father objected to her marryin' a plain farmin' feller like me and he put those cheap investigators on our tail when we ran away.'

Joanne backed up my barefaced lie with a sweet smile.

The youthful counterhand was won over and I thanked the powers that built a romantic soul under his homely face.

'Uh-huh,' he agreed and crossed to the window.

'Don't make it too obvious that you're on the look-out,' I cautioned.

He didn't. He deserves credit for having the interests of what he thought to be true love close to his heart.

'They're sittin' in the car right across from here,' he reported.

'Taking their time,' I groaned. 'They know we're in here and they'll have put a man at the back, too.'

Joanne gave me a startled look. I shoved my hand in the pocket of the coveralls and fondled the revolver.

Inside my skull, my brains ticked over. I figured I had the picture in its right perspective. The cop must have recovered, made it to a telephone and contacted his chief. That official would immediately contact Shelmerdine and, since the partisan police of Rollinsville could not wander this far off their own territory, Shelmerdine's torpedoes had been sent after us.

And here we were — trapped.

I wondered how soon we could expect help from Walt Toland and the Chicago agency boys who were somewhere in

Indiana on the look-out for us.

There were brains behind that counter-hand's docile front.

'I can get you out, even if there is a guy watchin' the back door,' he informed. He made that peculiar backward motion with the hand that railroad porters, cabmen and others with oddly flexible wrists are capable of on occasion.

I caught on and told him I could spare two dollars if his idea was good enough. I didn't tell him I wouldn't be able to pay him if it wasn't.

He had a good old-fashioned regard for money. His eyes lit up and he moved quickly away from the window.

'Listen,' he began, 'a pal of mine does some light truckin'. I can call him up and get him to call to the back door with his truck. There are some long fibre-board crates out in the kitchen, empty. It'll be a squeeze, but you could get into one each an' Chuck an' I will carry you out into the truck an' drive off. The guys who're watchin' will never know — two bucks in it for Chuck, too,' he added hastily.

'Two bucks in it for Chuck,' I agreed.

'Get busy, pal, those guys might be in a mood to wait all day — on the other hand they might come busting right in here and cause a scene.'

The counterhand crossed to the telephone booth.

He left the door wide open and we could hear him instructing Chuck. Chuck, too, must have shared his romantic soul, or maybe he just had the same regard for a couple of bucks. Either way, there seemed to be no argument from his end of the wire.

The white-coated youth came out of the booth.

'Chuck says okay,' he announced.

I pulled my billfold from the coveralls and eased out four greenbacks. 'For you and Chuck,' I said, handing them across. 'One more thing, do you have any wrapping paper and string?'

He moved back behind the counter, rooted underneath for a while and produced some stout wrapping paper and a length of grubby string.

'And a pen?' I asked.

'Pencil do?' he queried. I said it would.

I retired to a table well out of sight of the window. Watched by Joanne, I wrapped up the package of papers that were dynamite under the foundations of the Shelmerdine crime outfit and fastened the parcel with string. I addressed it to Walt Toland, care of World Investigations, Dearborn Avenue, Chicago, and wrote: 'Postage to be paid by addressee' in big letters across the spot where the stamp should go.

'The safest way of making sure mail gets delivered,' I told Joanne. 'Uncle Sam's mailmen are so eager to collect the money due for delivery that they never let an item addressed like that out of their sight.'

The counterhand went around the cafe ostensibly straightening up the tables, but keeping his weather eye out on the street.

'They're still sitting out there,' he reported.

'Playing the waiting game,' I grunted, 'and there'll be one or more out back.'

Business must have been slow with Chuck's trucking concern. He lost no time in arriving.

He was a beefy fellow, built like a tank. The notion of helping out a pair of eloping lovers seemed to appeal to him, he came through from the kitchen, grinning widely.

'Got the truck out back,' he greeted breezily. 'Had a hard time getting past a beat-up old hay-wagon some lame-brain left in the side alley — and there are a coupla funny looking guys loafing around out in the back area. How do you aim to get these love birds away, Fred?'

Fred gave a brief outline of his packing-case idea.

Chuck nodded. 'How far d'you want to go?' he asked.

'As far as your post-office first, then clear to Chicago,' I answered.

Chuck looked at his half of the four dollars Fred had split with him.

'There's more than two dollars in it for getting us to Chicago,' I said. 'First we want to get out of here, and stop off at the post-office.'

Chuck nodded agreement.

'Post-office is just along the street a ways. C'mon, let's go into our act.'

We trooped out into the kitchen, Joanne and I taking pains to keep out of sight of the street.

Fred was right about accommodation in the packing-cases being cramped.

They were long, fibre-board containers with close-fitting lids.

Joanne squeezed into one, lying flat, and the trucker and cafe man settled the lid into position. I climbed into a second one. It smelled strongly of something greasy. When Fred and Chuck fixed the lid into position, it was like being stowed in a coffin before your feet were cold.

They took Joanne out first, then came back for me.

'The two shamuses are still out back,' reported the voice of Fred the counter-hand through the thick texture of my coffin. They watched us take the first crate out, but don't seem to suspect anything.'

I felt the fibre-board coffin hoist into the air and make a swaying motion as it was carried out. It tilted down at one end as the pair descended some steps, then bumped heavily down on a wooden floor.

172

The slam and click of the truck door being fastened sounded and I shoved up against the lid and climbed out. Joanne's box was lying close by in the gloomy interior of the enclosed vehicle. I yanked off the lid and helped her out.

Up front Chuck hit the starter and the truck snorted into life.

'Don't know what we did to deserve the breaks, Mike,' said Joanne, 'but we seem to be getting them.'

'I'll feel better when we have these papers off our hands,' I answered. 'Putting them in the mail is about the best thing we can do with them in our present fix and the sooner we do that the better.'

Chuck negotiated the side-alley in which I had parked the old hay-truck. I glued my eye to the imperfect joining of the two doors. Through the crack, just as the truck turned out from the back of the restaurant, I caught sight of two of Shelmerdine's hoods leaning against a wall. One was the lean and hungry Slats, the second looked like the kid mobster who was in Shelmerdine's book-lined study the previous night.

The truck reached the main street and began a steady progression along its asphalted length. I pulled off the coveralls and stood in my shirt and pants, my suit jacket was still in the cab of the abandoned Ford truck.

Chuck jerked the truck to a halt and slid back the covering of the small square window which communicated the driver's cab and the rear of the truck.

'This is the post-office, right here,' he said.

I told Joanne to remain where she was and climbed out of the truck.

The post-office was a substantial brick building located at the corner of the main drag and a minor street. There was a big, wide-mouthed mailing-box standing close to the door of the building. All I had to do was walk a few yards, drop that package into the box and it was off my hands.

My feet touched the sun-sheened asphalt of the street and I started to walk towards the mailing box. Then, I heard the growl of a quickly-started car down the street at my back.

I whirled about. Down the straight length of the main street, I saw the Cadillac lunging forward from the kerb nearest the cafe. Two figures were running out of the alley in which I dumped the hay-truck. They wheeled on to the main street and came pounding the pavement in my direction.

The Cadillac was snorting up the sunlit street towards me. I could see Tescachelli's Italian face over the wheel.

So they had grown weary of waiting and entered the cafe. They had either forced the story of our escape from Fred or the truth about those packing-cases had dawned on them just naturally.

Anyway, they spotted me leaving the truck, saw me heading towards the post-office and were coming up-street — fast.

I started to run.

Only a matter of yards and I was at that mailing-box.

But the Cadillac was close upon me.

And the kid mobster across the street got trigger-happy.

He fired clear across the street as I started to run, I heard the slug whine past my ear and saw it chip the wall of the post-office.

Another universe away, a woman shrilled a high scream and a dog started to bark. I heard the car snort to a halt at the kerb.

I ran for the mail box the way a man runs from a horror in a nightmare, leaden-footed and seeming to move his legs on one spot without covering any ground.

Feet sounded behind me on the sidewalk.

And I made it by tossing the package the last yard, landing it into the safe-keeping of the United States Mail. I turned, saw Ike Tescachelli and another hoodlum only a matter of yards behind me, running with faces that portended trouble a-plenty.

A long way behind them, Slats and the trigger-happy kid were making across the street at a dead-run. An even longer way behind them, a figure in khaki uniform was blowing an urgent note on a police

176

whistle. One of the local cops, brought to life by the shot fired by the hot-headed young hood.

I made a swerve to run for the truck, but Tescachelli's pal made a grab at me. I swung about, tried to hit the hoodlum, but he got the first blow in and I went to the sidewalk, tasting the saltiness of blood.

The sidewalk was warm with the sun and the cop continued to blow his whistle in the distance. A cautious cop that, I thought. He was taking no chances on not making it across the years to his pension. He simply stood on one spot and blew his whistle.

The whole bundle of Shelmerdine mobsters piled on top of me, Tescachelli and his pal, joined by Slats and the trigger-eager kid.

I rolled on the sidewalk under their combined weight and they started slugging.

9

They could hand out a king-sized slugging, those Shelmerdine torpedoes, when they set their minds to it.

They hammered into me while I rolled on the hot sidewalk, with the far-away noise of an alarmed Stokestown sounding through a red haze. Somebody, I don't know who, was sprawled on top of me, somebody else was trying to drag me to my feet and a third somebody, with the temperament of a boxing kangaroo, kept swinging at my jaw and contacting every time.

I crooked my knees upwards and jabbed them hard into the belly of the hoodlum who was pinning me down. He gave a snorting gurgle and his weight shifted from me, then I got an arm free and began to swipe out blindly.

Whoever was trying to drag me upright almost succeeded, then I realised I was not alone in the fracas. I was getting help, good substantial help.

Chuck, the trucker, was wading into the thick of the fight with the power you'd expect from a guy built like a tank.

I came to my feet, half-dazed, and saw the truck driver deliver a haymaker across Ike Tescachelli's jaw. The mobster crumpled to the sidewalk. I saw the kid mobster, flourishing his clubbed heater, come out of nowhere and I put the flat of my hand square in his face and shoved him back, then I swung my other fist low and gave him the kind of blow that was good enough for his kind. He dropped his heater, doubled as if hinged in the middle and went scooting back on his heels.

Slats and the fourth hoodlum seemed to lose heart for the fight and went running for their car at the kerb.

I staggered around blindly for a couple of seconds flailing my fists. The cop was panting upstreet towards us, with another of the flatfoot breed alongside him.

Both were veterans and they couldn't run notably fast, but hadn't a great deal of distance to cover now. Tescachelli was beginning to sit up on the pavings and take interest in the world around him again. The youthful hoodlum was rolling around clutching his midriff and squawking.

Chuck grabbed my shoulder with a beefy fist.

'C'mon, let's get the hell out of here,' he suggested.

So we got the hell out of there. I could almost feel those two old country cops breathing on my neck as we ran for the truck.

We made it by the width of an eyelash.

Chuck pitched himself in behind the wheel and I slumped beside him. As he hit the starter and the truck jerked into life, I took a look at the street behind us. One cop was standing in the middle of the road, waving his arms like a windmill with St. Vitus' dance, the other was picking up Tescachelli. A crowd of Stokestown citizens stood around getting their eyes full of what was probably the most exciting spectacle the burg had witnessed since the night of the big wind.

Joanne Kilvert's face, wide-eyed and peaked, looked out of the communicating

180

window between the cab and the body of the truck.

One of my ears had stopped a hoodlum's fist and it felt three or four times too big. I rubbed it.

Chuck gunned the truck hard and it went roaring along the street to where a cluster of trees marked the vanishing point of the thoroughfare and the beginning of open country.

'Thanks for helping me out against those bums,' I told Chuck, 'but you shouldn't have done it. Drop us when you hit a lonely section of road.'

'Nuts, you said you wanted to go to Chicago and that's where I'll take you. I enjoyed that fight, but I didn't think those shamuses would get to using guns. That girl's father must hate you all to pieces.'

I remembered the piece of fiction I had concocted in the cafe. And this country cousin still believed it!

'Look, Chuck,' I said, 'those guys weren't private eyes and we're not eloping. They're Shelmerdine's monkeys — Athelstan Shelmerdine, ever heard of him?'

Chuck swallowed hard and looked at me sharply, then he concentrated his gaze on the country road ribboning ahead of the truck.

'Sure I've heard of him and I don't like the sound of him. Don't you still want to go to Chicago with me?'

Getting it through Chuck's skull was a man-sized job.

'Not after that little session of self-advertising in Stokestown,' I told him. 'The cops in that burg have had a good look at this vehicle and they'll have wired ahead to the highway patrols to intercept us. The Shelmerdine combine is not the only organisation on our tails, the cops are after me, too. Better drop us Chuck and we'll head across country on foot.'

Chuck kept the truck chugging along the tree-fringed road.

I was getting distinctly anxious. I took a quick look back, but saw no pursuing cars.

'What're the cops after you for?' asked Chuck.

'Ventilating a guy in South Bend, a mobster. It was self-defence — at least, I

182

shot to defend a pal of mine. I can clear up that mess after I've got the girl away from danger from the Shelmerdine crowd. Now, how about dropping us right here, before we run into trouble?'

'What do I do when I've dropped you? All Stokestown saw me fighting those guys with you, the cops, too. They'll ask questions.'

'Then you tell 'em lies,' I suggested. 'Tell 'em you were giving a couple of strangers a ride and when one of them stepped out at the post-office, he was attacked by hoodlums, so you went to his aid — don't tell them you know the hoodlums were Shelmerdine men and keep quiet about our being on the run.'

Chuck began to ruminate on that for a while. The truck was still eating up the road.

I began to crowd him.

'Chuck, Athelstan Shelmerdine is no gentle Annie. If his boys catch up with us — kkkk — kkk!' I drew my finger across my throat and clicked my tongue. 'And that goes for you, too.'

That won him over.

He braked at a spot where trees covered the road. He jerked his head towards a rail fence separating the road from pastureland.

'If you keep heading over those fields, you'll hit the state highway eventually. What do I do now, I can't go back to Stokestown until the heat cools off.'

'Keep heading the way you are, you might take the scent off us. I don't figure anyone will hurt you when they find we're not with you. Take a trip around the countryside until things cool off in your home town.'

I fumbled in my pants pocket, produced my wallet and fisted him a five dollar bill from my sadly dwindling roll.

'I wouldn't take it, but business is slack,' he apologised.

I turned to the window communicating with the back of the truck.

'End of the line, Joanne; from here on we walk.'

I stepped down and helped her out of the back of the truck.

We waved our good-byes to Chuck as he took the vehicle off up the road, climbed the rail fence and set off walking on the green grass.

There was no sign of traffic on the road.

I sniffed the air. It was sweet and clean.

'Seems a long way from mobsters and all their doings,' I observed.

'They won't stay too far away,' she replied. 'What happens now?'

'We keep walking until we reach the state highway, then get ourselves as far away from this vicinity as we can. I guess you'd best head for Chicago and the protection of World Wide, while I give myself up to the South Bend police and clear up the killing of Kornes.'

'What will they do, charge you?'

'Probably, but I shot to defend Jack Kay and that should help. We might stand a good chance of avoiding any further tangling with the Shelmerdine bunch, now. I guess the guardians of the law in that hick town back there will hold Tescachelli and his pals for a while after that fight on the street.'

Joanne pulled a wry face.

'Maybe there are more than Tescachelli

and those few men after us. Shelmerdine seems to be able to gather the clans pretty fast when he needs help from the underworld.'

'Yeah,' I grunted. 'But the Shelmerdine crowd isn't the only bunch running around the country. Walt Toland, my Chicago agency chief, and some of his boys are somewhere in the offing — I wish they'd meet up with us.'

We tramped over the fields for a long time, an oddly contrasting pair, I guess, Joanne in her crumpled summer dress, looking a little weary, but still mighty good, and me in shirt and pants, wearing a day's growth of beard. I felt like somebody who just got back from a New Year party lasting from January to July and my mouth tasted as if a herd of cattle had been driven through it.

My jacket was in the abandoned hay-wagon, the borrowed coveralls had been dumped in the rear of Chuck's truck. I had my wallet, the automatic and the Colt, taken from the cop in my trouser pockets and I was rid of the package of papers, which was a considerable relief.

'You're a good guy, Mike, getting me away from Shelmerdine's place the way you did last night and getting yourself mixed up in all this on my account,' Joanne said softly.

I made an attempt at a light-hearted laugh. It sounded like a rooster with tonsilitis trying out his morning song.

'Think nothing of it. I'm on vacation — having a wonderful time!'

'There's no telling what they would have done to me if you hadn't shown up,' she said.

'Athelstan did mention Lake Michigan,' I reminded her, 'which is as good a reason as any for making sure those hoodlums don't catch up with us again.'

We walked and walked.

Somewhere around noon, we reached the state highway. We plodded across a field and came to a white fence on the other side of which the wide banner of the highway stretched. Traffic was slack, just an occasional car or truck travelled the lanes.

Some distance from where we reached the highway, a signboard pointed north with the distances to Peru, Plymouth and South Bend marked upon it.

'That's our direction, girlie,' I said. 'Now, we have to set our minds to hitch-hiking, if any driver will give a ride to a leathery looking bum like me.'

I was also thinking about the cops who were combing Indiana for me, but didn't mention them.

We climbed the fence and started walking north along the grass margin of the highway. Every once in a while, when we heard an engine behind us, we turned and made hopeful expressions in the direction of the driver.

No takers.

Maybe it was me, coatless and with a blue-chin, that ruled us out as passengers. There was nothing in the least off-putting about Joanne.

We walked alongside the highway for about three-quarters of an hour. Joanne began to limp noticeably. The going had been rough for her, for she wore a pair of illogical high-heeled shoes, but she never complained.

'I wish I knew what those Rollinsville

cops did with my coupe after they slugged me with their clubs,' I complained.

A couple of slick cars zoomed up the north-bound lane, passing us like a couple of rich men ignoring two beggars by the roadside.

'I hope their tyres burst,' I snorted, watching the rear ends of the cars dwindling in the direction of Peru.

Another ten or fifteen minutes of walking and yet another motor sounded behind us. Joanne turned.

She clutched my arm suddenly, panicking.

'Mike, it's them!' she cried. 'That big car — it's Shelmerdine's!'

I whirled about and saw two cars coming up behind us. One was a powerful saloon, a big black monster with glittering trimmings, the second was smaller. In spite of the distance, I could see the legend lettered on a glass sign above the wind-shield: 'Rollinsville Police Department'.

I could see the uniformed chauffeur crouched over the wheel of the leading car. Both vehicles were eating up the asphalt.

I shoved my hand in my pants pocket, grabbed the handle of the Colt and held it there without drawing it out.

'C'mon,' I told Joanne, 'start running!'

We ran and the cars growled behind us like wild animals.

We kept running, although we knew we hadn't a chance. It was a kind of natural reaction, a dogged determination to keep moving until the bitter end, until the relentless pursuers caught up with us. We rounded a slight bend in the highway. There were a number of billboards at the margin of the road and close to them, a lone motor-cycle patrol-man.

'A cop,' I panted, 'we're on his territory and those Rollesville hawks are off theirs.' I grabbed the girl's arm, trying to pull her along faster. 'I'm going to give myself up to him and ask for police protection for you.'

The two big cars were at our backs, roaring. Up ahead, the state policeman saw us — two people running along the centre of the highway and a pair of powerful cars pursuing them. He gunned his engine and came roaring along in our direction.

Joanne and I panted to a halt. The two pursuing cars growled to a stop at our backs. The motor-cycle cop braked.

'What goes on?' he bawled. 'What's the big idea, running about the highway — ?' He took a long look at me. 'Hey, you're Lantry, the guy we're looking for! You shot a guy in South Bend!'

He swung out of the saddle of his machine and came stalking towards me. I was aware of figures emerging from the cars at our back.

'Yeah, I'm Lantry. Take me in. The girl, too!' I told him.

'Hold it, officer,' said a well-remembered voice behind me.

The fat chief of police from Rollinsville had stepped out of the police car and was walking towards us, waving a paper. 'I've got a warrant for these people.'

'He can't serve it here,' I objected. 'His police are off their jurisdiction, this is state jurisdiction, not Rollinsville.'

'Shut up,' said Chief Richards.

'What's the charge?' asked the patrol-man.

'Three charges. The major one is robbery — they took some of Mr. Shelmerdine's jewellery from the Shelm-erdine house last night.'

'That's a damn lie!' I yelled.

' — then there's a car stealing charge and one of assaulting a police officer and stealing his gun,' concluded Richards blandly.

In the bigger of the two cars, I could see Athelstan Shelmerdine lounging back in the cushions at the rear, smirking. The beefy sergeant of the Rollinsville police outfit and another of Shelmerdine's partisan flatfoots had emerged from the police car. Both stood in the background, fondling their revolvers.

'The girl is an accessory in each case,' went on Richards.

'These lugs can't take us in,' I howled at the patrolman. 'I'm wanted in South Bend in connection with homicide — that's more serious than the charges he's talking about — and that story about a jewel robbery is all lies.'

192

'You know the rules, officer, a municipal police force can arrest a wanted person on neighbouring jurisdictions when they can produce a warrant for them.'

'He's wanted in South Bend,' the officer pointed out.

'Sure, I'm wanted in South Bend,' I yelled at Richards, 'and I'm giving myself up to the state police.'

'Can you produce a warrant for either of these people?' the chief of Rollinsville police asked the motor-cycle cop.

'Why, no — '

'I can and it's quite in order for me to arrest both of them. You can inform your superiors they've been taken into custody by my force. The South Bend police will know where to find them — at Rollinsville.'

'I guess it's okay if you say so, sir,' said the state cop. 'Anyway, you have better means of arresting them right now.'

The Rollinsville sergeant and the other leather-jacketed cop advanced from the background.

'Good,' growled Richards. 'Better frisk

him — he's armed.'

The state cop frisked me and found the automatic and Colt, of course.

I caught a glimpse of Shelmerdine looking out of the window of his car.

'If you find a package on him, it contains the jewels taken from the Shelmerdine home and I'll take possession of it,' Richards said.

'No package,' reported the cop.

He looked quickly towards Joanne.

'You needn't frisk her,' I told him. 'She isn't carrying a handbag and if she had anywhere about her it would show, wouldn't it?'

The patrolman rubbed a hand over his mouth and surveyed Joanne's trim figure in the light summer dress.

'I guess it would,' he agreed.

The two uniformed cops from Rollinsville closed in on us, showing us the inside of their gun muzzles.

The sergeant grabbed me by the arm and began to shove me towards the police car. I whirled around to face the state cop.

'Listen, O'Flaherty,' I bellowed, 'you

194

make sure the South Bend dicks pull us out of Rollinsville pretty damn quick. Make sure of that!'

'C'mon,' snarled the poor man's Marlon Brando, yanking at my arm.

'Lake Michigan,' I thought, 'here we come!'

10

They bundled Joanne and myself into the roomy back compartment of the police car, the sergeant sitting on one side of us, Richards on the other, and the third cop drove.

Leaving the motor-cycle cop to watch our departure, both cars swung about to face the south and started back for Shelmerdine's cosy mansion with the police vehicle leading.

'Where's the package you took from Mr. Shelmerdine's house last night?' growled Richards.

'Find out,' I told him.

'We will. What did you do with it?'

'Ask Ike Tescachelli.'

'Wise guy! Tescachelli isn't around. We understand the sheriff's department at Stokestown is holding him and his pals for civil disturbance.'

'Good. I hope they hold 'em for a long, long time.'

'They won't.'

'Your bunch will pull strings, I suppose.'

'Something like that. What did you do with it?'

'With what?'

'The package — don't act dumb!'

'I'm not acting. I was born dumb. I must have been or I wouldn't be in this fix.'

'What did you do with the package?'

'This is where I came in. Ask Tescachelli next time you see him. Let's change the subject, Fatso, what are you going to do when the South Bend cops come looking for the girl and me?'

'Give 'em two stiffs, you both know too much!'

I thought about that for a long time.

Then I said: 'I was born dumb, like I said, so you'll have to explain. The South Bend dicks will ask questions about how we got stiff. Asking questions is an occupational disease of coppers — real coppers, I mean — what will you tell them?'

'We'll tell them how two people armed

themselves with stolen guns and busted out of the Rollinsville police headquarters. Only one thing policemen can do when they're dealing with desperate and armed escapees.'

'And you'll claim we were shot in self-defence, of course.'

'In defence of the community and ourselves — always the community before self. We'll make it look awful good.'

Richards cast a glance at Joanne Kilvert's blanched features.

'It's a pity about the girl, though,' he added.

'You want to watch those scruples, Richards,' I told him. 'One of these times, you'll find yourself spending a night hanging over the bathroom bowl spilling your innards because of some everyday thing like shooting an old lady.'

Inwardly, I was very close to panic.

I realised I could not tell these Shelmerdine partisans that I had put the package in the mail and that it would be on the way to Chicago by now. Once these strong-arm artists realised the game was nearly up, they would have no hesitation in killing us out of revenge I was going to have to play it very carefully, for the girl's sake.

The police car was still travelling along the highway in front of Athelstan Shelmerdine's plutocrat's wagon. Suddenly, it turned off the highway on to a smaller branch road that would take us into Shelmerdine's home-territory.

I was still thinking furiously.

Richards was talking:

'You better play smart, Lantry, we'll find out what you did with the papers sooner or later and we'll find out the hard way — hard for you, that is. If you dumped them along the way, we'll get them. We know all your moves since you jumped it from Mr. Shelmerdine's house, thanks to your own stupidity. That cop you hit legged it to the Whitley farm as soon as he was fit. He made the people there talk and he called me, telling me everything.'

'He was lucky,' I said. 'That big-mouthed Mrs. Kunitz was hogging the wire when I tried.'

Richards looked at me fish-eyed. He

didn't know what I was talking about.

'We know all about the car you pushed into the pond and the hay truck you took from the farm,' he went on.

'So that's how Tescachelli and his mugs tracked us down to Stokestown,' I said. 'You found out about those things, Richards, why not try finding out about the package of papers by using your own natural-born acumen.'

Richards began to lose his temper. He started to make a motion in the direction of the heater in its shoulder-holster under his jacket. On the far side of the seat, the sergeant was rubbing a finger up and down the club fastened at his belt.

'Better come across with the whereabouts of that package, Lantry,' Richards snorted. 'Or we'll get it out of you the hard way.'

'Nuts,' I said. 'You two puppets wouldn't dare make a move until the puppet-master pulls your strings and he's riding in the car behind you.'

'Better give with the information,' blustered Richards.

'Horse-radish!' I told him.

The car which carried Shelmerdine began to honk its horn behind us.

I turned about and looked out of the rear window. The chauffeur of the car behind was signalling with his hand. We were travelling along a lonely and obviously little-used dirt-road.

'Slow down, Tonks,' Richards ordered the cop who was driving, 'Mr. Shelmerdine's car is going to overtake.'

The cop cut speed and pulled into the side of the road. Shelmerdine's chauffeur gunned the big luxury model and swept past the police vehicle. Tonks pulled the police car behind it and we travelled along in its wake.

Richards began to get tough again.

I wondered where the blazes Walt Toland and the Chicago boys were hiding themselves.

'Where's the package?' asked Richards.

'That's the twenty-eleventh time you've squawked that tune, Richards,' I replied. 'Why don't you shut up?'

Richards growled and the beefy police sergeant glowered at me.

Up ahead, Shelmerdine's car slowed

down and the driver was signalling again. He began making a turn into a gate giving on to a roadside meadow.

'Where's he going?' the driver of the police car wanted to know.

'Follow him,' rasped Richards curtly. 'Mr. Shelmerdine knows best.'

Tonks, the cop at the wheel, swung the car to follow the chauffeur-driven one through the gate in the fence and along a rugged path that caused the car to jounce heavily.

The path was little more than a cart-track. The police vehicle kept right after it until the track dwindled away to a mere hair-line. High trees swept upwards on all sides, hiding the place from the road. The chauffeur of Shelmerdine's car braked the vehicle, Tonks followed suit.

Out of the car came the obese form of Shelmerdine, followed by his chauffeur, a smooth-featured youngster in a black uniform and visored cap.

Shelmerdine motioned a finger at our car and his puppets inside it jumped into action. Richards handed me a dig in the ribs.

'Outside — both of you,' he said.

We got out, so did Richards and his leather-coated cops. I didn't like the set-up one little bit. The place was quiet and tree-shaded, a long way from anywhere. The sort of location in which you could have your teeth kicked out of your head and nobody would hear you yelling.

They clustered around us, all of them, the chauffeur, Richards, the sergeant, the cop named Tonks, and Athelstan Shelmerdine who held the stage.

Joanne and I were in the centre of them.

'Where's the package, Lantry?' Shelmerdine asked.

The others adopted threatening attitudes.

'Find out,' I said.

A reasonable impression of a smile — a shark's smile — spread over Shelmerdine's flabby face. He stroked his clipped moustache with the tip of a neatly manicured finger.

'Your attitude is most foolish, Lantry,' he said. 'You can either tell us voluntarily or we'll find out by — er — somewhat uncivilised methods.'

'Nuts, Shelmerdine, Richards has been squawking that tune into my ear for the past fifteen minutes.'

I took a quick look around. The two uniformed cops from Rollinsville had their hands on their kingsize clubs. I didn't like that.

There was a cluster of small rocks lying on the ground close to the bole of a tree about five yards from where I stood. I wondered vaguely what my chances were of getting my hands on one of them to use as a weapon.

'I'm not satisfied that one or the other of you hasn't got the package hidden about you,' Shelmerdine was saying. 'I think a thorough search of Mr. Lantry is called for.'

'You won't find any package on me, Shelmerdine,' I told him.

'Then we'll search the girl.'

Off to one side, the young chauffeur inched back the corners of his mouth into a hard grin and said: 'Heh, heh.'

'You'll keep your grubby mitts off her,'

I told Shelmerdine.

It was Shelmerdine's turn to say, 'Heh, heh,' and he did.

Then he inclined his head towards me. 'Frisk him,' he ordered.

They closed in on me, all of them, Richards, the two uniformed policemen and the chauffeur. I kept my eyes on the clutter of handy-sized rocks.

A hand grabbed me by the shoulder but I jumped forward and broke free of the grip. I saw a face before me, that of Tonks, the Rollinsville cop. I figured I could at least lessen the odds by one, so I swung out at him hitting his jaw hard, and got a kind of brief and detached satisfaction out of watching him crumple down. Then I was grabbed again, I started to struggle, somebody hit me a hard swipe across the back of the neck. This sent me staggering forward, half-blinded, to hit the ground on my stomach.

Dimly, I was aware that I was now lying close to the clutter of rocks, I made a grab for one, rolled over on to my back, clutching the rock.

I had a crazy, whirling impression of

Richards, the sergeant and the chauffeur bearing down on me. Shelmerdine was standing off to one side yelling something, but I couldn't appreciate what it was.

The Shelmerdine hoodlums piled on to me. The police sergeant had his club drawn and he handed a hefty smack across my shoulders. I felt the combined weight of the three men pressing me down to the hard ground. Through a streaky haze of salt tears I could hear Shelmerdine yipping. I gathered he was telling the others to keep me conscious. Of course he wanted me conscious. Unconscious, I could not tell him what had happened to that all-important bundle of papers.

They pounded and pummelled and pinned me down, but I kept a grip on the rock. I managed to hang on to it as I slithered into a dizzying haze. It was like a solid anchorage and I kept hanging on to it as they rolled me on the ground and threw their fists at me.

They started to hoist me up to my feet. I guess they figured I was through offering resistance and they could search me without any further trouble. But I still had the rock clutched in my hand, a comforting lump of hardness between my fingers.

I couldn't see properly, but their hands were beginning to pluck at my clothing. I shook my head, foucussed my vision and wobbled like a drunk.

They were starting in to search me, all three of them, going at it as if they didn't care if they ripped every stitch of clothing off my back. I guess they didn't, at that.

But I still had my rock.

I waited just long enough to get a breath of air into my lungs.

Then I swung out with the rock.

I gave it to Chief Richards first, right above the ear. I don't like crooked cops, so I put all the beef I could swing into the blow.

Richards went down without a sound.

The big sergeant said: 'Why, you — '

Then I saw his club, coming up before my eyes. I ducked, swung out a feeble blow with the rock. The chauffeur was trying to claw at me. He was near enough for me to kick him, so I did, hard on the shin. He yelled and loosened his grip.

The Rollinsville police sergeant swung out a blow with his club, swiping me on the side of the head. I reeled, recovered my balance, saw him coming for me again and pitched the rock at him. It hit him in the chest, slowed him down, but did not stop his progression towards me. The broad face was set in determined lines and his knuckles showed white on the grip of the club. The youthful chauffeur had recovered from his kicked shin and he was advancing on me, too.

I was half-dazed. I had lost my rock and had only my bare hands to fight them off with. The cop hit me a crack with his club, a hard blow this time, very much in the tradition of the hammering he and his pals gave me on the road outside Rollinsville.

A muzzy haze began to close in on me. I figured I'd had my run of luck, but I fought hard to keep conscious.

Then I saw a flurry of brightly flowered material behind the cop, just as he raised the club for another blow. I heard

Shelmerdine's wheezy voice shout something. He sounded so far away he could have been somewhere in the middle of Arkansas.

I was so stupid as a result of the recent clubbing, I only half appreciated what happened next. All I knew was that the police sergeant went down like a pole-axed bull and the blow he had raised his club for never landed.

That gave me the fillip I needed to rise above the waves of unconsciousness that were threatening to engulf me. I shook my head and brought my vision into something close to correct focus.

I was aware of the big carcass of the cop lying at my feet. The slim form of the black uniformed chauffeur was sprawled close to him, twitching slightly like a fly that had been swatted hard enough to knock the buzz, but not the life, out of him.

I staggered around a little with a pair of legs that only half belonged to me and almost fell off them when I caught sight of the fly swatter and who had done the swatting.

Joanne Kilvert was standing back against one of the parked cars. In one hand, she held a police baton, taken from Tonks, who was now sitting on the grass, feeling the jaw I had slugged, in the other she had an Army Colt, held to cover Tonks, the semi-conscious chauffeur, Richards and the sergeant, both out cold, and Athelstan Shelmerdine.

Shelmerdine was a picture. He was up against the bole of a tree, dithering visibly. His complexion was as yellow as a snake's belly and he had suddenly become an old, old man. He held one hand up to his face and a thin thread of blood was creeping down towards his chin.

Joanne stood her ground, holding the big Colt firmly, looking like Calamity Jane in modern dress.

'When you hit the policeman first, I managed to get his gun while he was unconscious,' she explained. 'Shelmerdine tried to stop me, but I scratched him across the face, then I took the policeman's club and hit the sergeant and Cortines, the chauffeur.'

I think I managed a grin. I know I quoted Kipling.

' 'The female of the species', Shelmerdine, don't think this girl won't have nerve enough to shoot if anyone gets smart, she will. She has plenty of cause to trigger your torpedoes, too, your Miss Jones is the sister of Arthur Kilvert, the man who stood up to your lousy trade union grafting.'

Athelstan Shelmerdine, the mogul of the rackets, looked something akin to a deflated balloon. I got a great kick out of seeing him so.

Joanne kept the mobsters covered while I made a quick round of the wounded. I took the Army Colt from the belt of the unconscious sergeant, another from Richards' shoulder holster and the chauffeur proved to have a wicked little derringer in the pocket of his tunic.

I shoved the derringer into my pants pocket, handed one of the Colts to Joanne and kept the other rammed into Shelmerdine's paunch while I frisked him.

He didn't have a weapon.

'Got so respectable you don't carry a

heater any more, eh, Athelstan?' I sneered, 'but why should you when you can get stupid lugs like these to do your gunning for you?'

Shelmerdine said nothing, he simply stood there and quivered.

'Keep your eye on 'em a little while longer, Two-gun Katie,' I told Joanne. I crossed to the car belonging to the Rollinsville Police Department, lifted the hood and snapped every connection I could break with my bare hands. Then, for good measure, I pulled the valves out of both rear tyres and watched the car flop down on to the rims. Then I pitched the valves into the long grass.

Tonks was still sitting on the grass, rubbing his jaw; the chauffeur was easing himself painfully into a sitting position; the sergeant was still out cold, but Richards was beginning to twitch. Shelmerdine was still standing against the tree, looking like a pricked balloon the colour of last month's cheese.

I hoisted Cortines, the chauffeur, to his feet, none too gently, stripped him of his black, high collared tunic and buttoned it on my own coatless torso. It was a pretty good fit and it covered the shirt that the hoodlums had reduced almost to ribbons. I jammed the cap on my head.

'I hope I don't catch any of your body-population,' I told him and I dropped him. He hit the ground limply like a sack of wet sand.

I faced Shelmerdine and offered him a word of advice.

'Shelmerdine, you're through. The package of papers will be in the hands of the Crime Commission in a matter of days now, and I'm not bluffing this time. Your day as the big string-puller is over. Go home and shoot yourself — save the taxpayers the expense of feeding you in jail.'

Joanne and I, keeping the Colts levelled, backed towards the big car belonging to Shelmerdine.

It was quite a car, further proof that crime pays in material things if not in peace of mind. Inside, it was just a shade smaller than Carnegie Hall. Joanne seated herself in the off-side seat and placed her two Colts in the glove compartment.

I sank into the driver's seat and hit the starter.

We left the battlefield.

I took a backward glance at Shelmerdine as I gunned the big car along the rutted track.

He was standing against the tree, surveying his injured strong-arms.

He looked very weary, very flabby and very old.

I almost felt sorry for him.

11

Out of the gate, along the dirt road to the highway and then northward, I drove the powerful car.

'Still going to give yourself up to the police?' Joanne asked, as we streaked up the ribbon of highway in the direction of Peru.

'I don't know, I've been thinking about it. I want to clear up that killing for the sake of Jack and Beth Kay, but I want to see you safe in Chicago first. When the Crime Commission gets round to investigating those papers, we'll be key witnesses. I'm half inclined to make a run for it, through South Bend and clear up to Chicago and risk being picked up. This chauffeur's get-up will help to cover my identity and the cops will have quit searching for me now, under the impression I'm in the custody of those so-called policemen at Rollinsville.'

I weighed the situation in silence for

awhile. Most of all, I wanted to get Joanne clear away from any danger from the Shelmerdine combine. I didn't figure on Athelstan Shelmerdine staying a pricked balloon for long. He may or may not have believed my story about the papers being on the way to the Crime Commission but, either way, as his man Richards pointed out earlier, we both knew far too much.

In Shelmerdine's book, we were marked for the rub-out treatment.

'Yes,' I said, 'we'll make a run for it, and risk the consequences. Little Miss Two-gun Katie has had a busy time riding the range. I guess it's about time she headed home and spent a peaceful night tucked up in little old Chicago.'

She smiled.

'You're okay, Lantry, did anyone ever tell you that?'

That made me feel uncomfortable. I blushed. Me — Mike Lantry!

'Lay off, Joanne. I bet you tell that to all the private eyes who run around with holes in their heads.'

'No, I mean it, Mike. At first I thought

you were extra-hard, extra-tough and extra-cynical. I thought you were efficient but the kind of life a man like you would lead would make you not very nice to know. I was wrong — you're okay.'

'Lay off, you're getting under the chinks in my armour.'

I turned my head away and concentrated on the road in order to avoid her elfin face. A face like that, cute as a chocolate cake, could grow on a man if he let it get a good grip on him.

There was a packet of cigarettes in the driver's glove compartment. They must have been the chauffeur's, but they were a good brand. I took them and gave one to the girl.

'Let's smoke, by way of changing the subject,' I suggested.

'Okay. The subject's changed. Give me a light.'

There was a dashboard lighter from which we lit our cigarettes.

We smoked in silence for some time while the big car zoomed up the highway. Shortly before reaching Peru, we passed a lone motor cycle patrolman sitting his machine at the side of the highway. He gave us the merest of passing glances.

On the outskirts of Peru there was a diner where we stopped for a meal of french-fried potatoes, fish and coffee. It was rough grub, prepared for a clientele of truckers, but it tasted like ambrosia to me. The diner had a washroom where I cleaned up my battered face. I needed a shave badly and when I looked into the mirror, I realised I didn't quite fill the part of a chauffeur. Nobody in the diner seemed to care about that, they didn't even appear to notice that my coat and pants weren't made for each other.

I had Walt Toland and the boys from the Chicago branch of World Wide on my mind. The only way I could contact them was by calling the Chicago office which was in touch with them by radio transmitter. By this time I guessed they would be somewhere around the Stokestown area. The diner didn't have a telephone, which annoyed me, so I couldn't contact Chicago.

I stalked out and met Joanne at the car. She had done some smartening up in the ladies' washroom. She looked cuter than two chocolate cakes now.

We hummed into Peru.

In that single-street town, I found the post-office and called Chicago.

O'Toole answered.

'O'Toole, this is Lantry. Are you still in radio contact with Walt and his boys?'

'Yes.'

'Well, where are they?'

'Somewhere in the region of Stokestown. They say they drew a blank at the Shelmerdine home, chief. They busted in, looking for you and the girl, but the whole place was empty but for a woman and a kid.'

'Then what?'

'Then they headed for Stokestown after they got your earlier message. They did some snooping around and found a trucker, Chuck somebody-or-other, who told them you'd been there and got in a fight on the street. He showed them a place on the road where he dropped you and the girl.'

'And where are they now?'

'Still combing around that section of

Indiana, I guess.'

'Well, get in touch with them again and tell them to quit combing. They would have been useful while the girl and I were battling the whole Shelmerdine combine with our bare hands, but now they're merely wasting gasoline for which World Wide is paying. Tell 'em we're in Peru, heading home. I've got news for you and them, O'Toole. There's a package in the mail addressed to you and that means the Shelmerdine bunch is on its way out for keeps.'

O'Toole made a noise of appreciation.

'Are you safe?' he asked. 'Are you out of danger?'

'Reasonably so, I guess. A country sheriff has clawed in some of the smaller fry of the Shelmerdine shock-troops, while the big boss and some others are stranded in rural America with a jimmied car. Tell Walt and the others to head for home.'

'Okay,' agreed O'Toole.

I thought of Walt and his boys running around the Indiana countryside half-cocked. They were good guys, all of them, and couldn't really be blamed for failing to pick up the erratic trail the girl and I had left during the previous few hours.

'Private dicks!' I said to myself, imitating the scornful tones of Chief Richards.

Back in the car with Joanne, I started up and headed out of Peru. We made good going, it was pleasant travelling that stretch of highway over the flat land between Peru and Plymouth.

Evening came sifting down slowly as we approached Plymouth. I began to get a little less edgy. Cops we passed on the way did not pay any attention to me. I began to forget I was a hunted man.

I would take the girl to Chicago tonight, make sure she was safe and done with all this hectic rushing around the country, then I would contact the police at South Bend and clear up the business of my shooting Speedy Kornes.

We passed the spot where I first found Joanne walking in the rain, on past the dirt-road where I turned to avoid the pursuing Shelmerdine hoods. It all seemed so long ago in the past, now.

Night shrouded the land as we passed the hoarding into which the hoodlum's car had crashed. The grinning woman on the billboard still advertised somebody's toothpaste, but the wreck of the gangsters' sedan had gone.

We reached Plymouth, threaded our way through the lighted streets, emerged and headed north for South Bend, with its bitter associations.

We smoked the remainder of the chauffeur's cigarettes, chatted some, then Joanne fell asleep.

I had seen her asleep before. Each time she had reminded me of an unprotected little kid. She reminded me of a little kid that first night, a few miles back there, in the trees around the dirt-road where we hid from the gunmen close behind. Right now, she was like a child, curled up on the soft seat of the car that Athelstan Shelmerdine could afford out of the dirty money he had amassed over the years of full-time thievery. She was a far cry from the spirited young woman who went into action earlier that day with a cop's club and an Army Colt, but she didn't look scared any more.

She seemed contented, resting peace-fully.

She thought I was okay.

And that was a compliment.

The lights of South Bend came over the horizon, distant, glittering stars, multi-coloured.

I steered towards them remembering the first night I drove towards them in the company of Joanne Kilvert. I remembered how I reflected on the way a spangled cloak of lights can hide the filth of a city. I remembered what I left behind me the last time I saw South Bend, a dead man, bullet-pounded on the lawn of one of my best friends.

That was ugly.

A rotten business. I had gone into the home of two fine people and something from the dirty world I moved in followed in my wake.

I would never be able to apologise enough to Beth and Jack for what happened that Sunday morning.

I brightened with the thought that my shooting the pock-marked little hood was

223

better than his putting a bullet through Jack, which was what he was fixing to do when I fired on him.

Joanne still slept.

Past the city-limit signs and on towards the heart of South Bend I gunned the car.

The lights of the city flashed past. I began to wonder if Codfish the Cop would be anywhere around to recognise me and I was grateful for the visored chauffeur's cap that served to shade my face.

I was on the centre of Michigan Street when I first suspected I was being tailed. A small car, open, with three or four dark blobs of humanity in it, was sticking close to my tail. Maybe I was too jittery, I thought. It's not notably unusual to have a car at your back for a considerable length of time on a busy thoroughfare of a city.

A second car slithered out of a side-turning and fell in behind the one on my tail. It was a large sedan.

I didn't care for the pattern of all this.

I decided to try them.

At the junction of Monroe Street I

made a right turn. The two cars, keeping the same measured distance behind me, followed. I kept on along Monroe until I reached the crossing of Main Street, turned into Main Street, with one eye on the mirror.

They came after me, keeping the same distance, unhurried.

I gunned the car. So did the drivers at my back.

I tried desperately to recollect my South Bend geography, hit the gas even harder and did a quick round-trip of several blocks: Colfax Avenue, Taylor Street, Western Avenue, across the intersection of Lafayette Street and on towards Michigan again.

The speed of the car woke Joanne.

'What's happening?' she asked, sleepily.

'I think we're being tailed, but I'm not sure. Two cars. I've lost them, now.'

Her face blanched.

'I thought we were free of trouble,' she said.

'So did I. I was getting too complacent. It might have been pure coincidence that those cars went everywhere I did, on the other hand, it might not.'

I turned left off Western and on to Michigan.

The road behind was clear, but I was still uneasy. I might have given them the slip, but maybe they were playing a crafty game of hide-and-seek.

I kept hitting a fair lick clear through South Bend. Just before hitting the north-bound highway out of the city, Joanne nudged me.

'There are two cars staying close behind us,' she said. 'Can you see them?'

'I've seen them for a long time,' I told her. 'They picked us up on Michigan again. If you look closely, you'll see a third car some distance behind the first two, I think he's one of the pack, too.'

'But how have they done it?' the girl wanted to know. 'Shelmerdine and the others couldn't possibly have caught up with us — or are they police who recognised you?'

'Not police — another bundle of Shelmerdine's cats-paws. He pulls strings in the underworld of the whole of this section of the map. I suppose he's contacted some of his puppets among the less respectable citizens of South Bend and told them to watch out for and tail us. I don't like it, Joanne. If Shelmerdine's convinced I told him the truth about getting rid of those papers, he has nothing to lose and he won't hesitate to give his hoods the high-sign to finish us off — Chicago style.'

She clutched my arm and glanced with fear-fraught eyes at the dark shapes of the pursuing cars.

'What can we do, Mike? We're in open country now, they can catch up with us and start shooting.'

I eyed the pursuing cars in the mirror. Three of them, keeping an even distance each behind the other and the first of them about two hundred yards behind our car.

'Catching up with a high-powered bus like this is a man-sized job,' I replied, 'when I pull the throttle out, like this!'

I gave Shelmerdine's plutocrat's wagon everything under the hood and it went rocketing up the darkened highway with dizzying speed.

'I think we can shake those leeches off with a series of quick bursts like this, they can't match this speed. We'll make a dead-run for Chicago and let's hope we don't meet up with any police patrols because I intend to break the limit considerably tonight.'

I kept on gunning the car and the three cars at our back dwindled. I slackened speed again for a time, then jerked the big vehicle into another spurt.

There was no sign of the three following cars now.

Joanne pointed to a distant glitter of lights, reflected in far-off water sheened by the fitful moon.

'The lake,' she said, 'we got this near to Chicago without trouble, at least.'

'Yeah,' I answered, watching the distant shine of Lake Michigan, 'but we still have a lot of ground to travel; Gary, East Chicago and Hammond. If Shelmerdine has any dogs in those towns, he might have called them up, which means we'll have a sizeable pack to dodge.'

I drove in silence for a long time, keeping a watch on the mirror for indications of the pursuing vehicles. Only the dark sweep of the highway was visible at our backs.

Along the margin of Lake Michigan, the highway was a dark, straight stretch of asphalt, occasionally illuminated by the fugitive moon.

The distant lights of Gary came into sight.

I slackened speed, feeling sure that we had put the pursuers well behind us. Joanne struck a listening attitude, her brow clouded suddenly.

'Mike! I can hear a sound over the engine — I don't like it — listen!'

I listened. Over the regular note of the purring motor, I heard a steady, whirring beat.

Joanne wound her window down quickly. Air, chilled by the nearness of the lake, seeped into the interior of the big auto. The girl leaned out, looking upward anxiously.

She pulled her head back into the car and turned to me with frightened features.

'Mike. There's a helicopter above us!'

12

That numbed me.

'A helicopter?'

'Yes, it's Shelmerdine, Mike. He had a 'copter at the Rollinsville mansion, Greg Cortines, the chauffeur, pilots it. Could they have caught up with us this soon in the 'copter?'

'Yes, easily when you consider we lost some time by having a meal and in trying to shake off those tails in South Bend.'

The whirring tune of the flying machine's blades came through the open window. It sounded like the flapping wings of the angel of death.

Joanne began to grow pessimistic.

'We're sunk, Mike, we can't shake them off. They can cling to us for miles, even come down low and shoot at us!'

'They can float close to us in open country, girlie, but they'll have to take that flying egg-whisk high over a town.

That's Gary right ahead. Watch my smoke!'

I gave the big car the gun and kept right on raising the speed needle until we passed the Gary limit signs, then I slowed a little and headed for the centre of the town.

Joanne was leaning from the window.

'I can still see them,' she reported. 'They're a long way behind, coming after us.'

I plunged the car into the built-up centre of Gary, like a rabbit making for a warren. Joanne was keeping watch on what small portion of sky was visible between the tops of the buildings as I drove along the central street.

'Can't see the helicopter now,' she told me.

In the driving mirror, I saw what I half-expected to see when we reached Gary. A black saloon slinking out of a side-street behind the car I was driving, to fall into a steady pursuit.

Another tail. Shelmerdine must have been mighty busy since we left him in that field. I had little doubt he had called up his strong-arm contacts in every town on the way to Chicago. Now, we had the two tails from South Bend somewhere at our backs, the helicopter somewhere in the sky and this Johnny-come-lately close behind.

The odds were thickening and the Shelmerdine dogs were out with a vengeance.

I didn't mention the new bloodhound to Joanne, but she spotted him.

'Another car following us, Mike,' she said quietly. 'It's like you said, Shelmerdine catspaws waiting to pick up our trail all along the way.'

We were reaching the outskirts of Gary. I shoved the throttle wide open and streaked for the open road.

'What are our chances, Mike?' Joanne asked in a quiet, even voice.

'Great,' I lied, 'but check the cylinders of those two Colts in your glove compartment. Two-gun Katie may have to ride again before tonight's out.'

She took the pair of revolvers from the compartment, flipped open the cylinders.

'Both fully loaded.'

'Good, keep them close to hand.'

I took one hand from the wheel, fished the third Army Colt from my pocket and checked the cylinder. Fully loaded.

In the mirror, the tailing saloon was still visible, coming along behind us on the wide road with its lights dimmed. Joanne Kilvert took another glance at the sky.

'The helicopter's in view again,' she commented. 'A long way up, but coming down and they must have spotted us!'

I gave the car the gun once again.

'East Chicago, here we come,' I said without feeling in the least enthusiastic.

'And I suppose more of Shelmerdine's men will be waiting there to join the chase,' she remarked.

'I wouldn't be surprised.'

I shoved the accelerator down to the floor, kicked every ounce of power out of the big auto. A coughing note crept into the hum of the motor.

I watched the gasoline needle, feeling far from happy.

'Do you believe in old sayings like

'Trouble never comes alone'?' I asked Joanne.

'Can't say I've paid much attention to them.'

'Nor did I, until now, but I'll make them my life's study if we ever get out of this fix, girlie. We're running out of gas.'

'Oh, no!'

'Oh, yes! It's not so surprising. I've been gunning this big heap like an Indianapolis track driver.'

Joanne cast her eyes upwards. Both of us could hear the mounting whirr of the 'copter's vanes. And the black saloon became a little larger in the driving mirror.

There must have been plenty of guys feeling happier than me right then. I had to think fast and thinking can hurt when your head has more or less got used to being a target for crooked cops' clubs the way mine had of late.

The car that was tailing us grew a little bigger in the mirror; the tune of the helicopter's prop grew a little louder; the motor of the big car began to splutter again.

Up ahead, the lights of East Chicago glittered in the night.

'Listen,' I told Joanne, 'East Chicago is only a little way ahead and there's just enough gas to make it, I guess. I'm going to jump from the car just before we come to that cluster of trees, up ahead and to the left. I'll run for the trees and try to attract attention to myself. You give the car everything it's got and use that last drop of gas to reach East Chicago. When you make it, find a telephone. Ask for Chicago and get World Wide Investigations. O'Toole will be off duty by now, but tell whoever answers to get into radio contact with Walt Toland and his boys and tell them I tried to draw the Shelmerdine bloodhounds into the woods between Gary and East Chicago. They're supposed to be headed for Chicago out of Indiana. Tell World Wide to instruct them to come out here fast and looking for trouble.'

'But, you can't fight alone!' she protested.

'No, but I can give them a run for their money, and hold off the chase while you run for East Chicago and the telephone. Now, change seats with me, slow down until I jump clear then gun it for those lights ahead. Okay?'

'Okay,' she agreed reluctantly.

We changed seats. It was easy to do so in a car just a shade less than the size of Carnegie Hall.

I grabbed one of the Colts from the glove compartment, leaving her the other.

'It's Two-gun Mike's night to ride,' I told her. 'Slacken speed until I jump.'

I took a last look in the mirror and saw the saloon, very much bigger. The flying egg-whisk was whirring loudly above us.

Cold air, touched with the smell of smoke, drifting over from the smoke-stacks of East Chicago's heavy industrial plants, seeped into the car as I opened the door. I held one Colt in my hand, the second was in my pocket.

Joanne dropped speed. The engine was rasping nastily.

'Good luck!' she shouted.

'Give 'er the gun!' I yelled.

And I jumped.

I hit the road with a jolt that jarred

every bone in my body, but managed to keep upright. I had a brief impression of something floating in the night air with a whirring airscrew spinning above it; the black saloon was closer than I thought, roaring up the highway towards me.

At my back, Joanne speeded the erratic motor of the big car and I heard it go zooming away. Over to the far side of the road, was a grass slope, topped by the stand of dark trees that I intended to make for.

I turned, half-crouched in the roadway and fired at the oncoming car, shooting low at the front wheels. The vehicle veered crazily across the highway, broad-side on and with a screaming of brakes.

I started running in a zig-zag for the rising grassland and the trees, vaguely aware of the whirring helicopter swinging off course and dropping lower. As I ran, I took a quick look over my shoulder, saw that Joanne was streaking away into the distance.

The saloon had stopped and dark figures were spilling out, the flying-machine was coming lower. My shooting at the car had resulted in precisely the effect I had played for — attention had been diverted from the girl. I decided to keep it that way and pegged a shot up at the flying egg-whisk. Then, I was on the grass of the slope, running hard, feeling springy turf under the soles of my Oxfords.

I wasn't prepared for the way in which the men in the helicopter answered my shot. A repetitive crackle of machine-gun fire sounded from the sky.

I doubled almost in two and kept running upwards to the trees. I guess I was a poor target from the air, running against the black mass of the grassy slope, but I heard the bullets thumping into the earth only a matter of feet behind my heels.

Down on the highway, the dark figures from the car that had tailed us out of Gary were giving chase. Somebody blasted a shot at me, but the slug went whining above my head.

I kept running, zig-zagging, slithering on the dew-wet grass, making for the stand of shadowed trees at the crest of the rise.

My heart was pounding like a trip-hammer.

Feet thumped on the grass behind me; the spinning vanes of the 'copter's propeller sounded closer. Another splutter of automatic fire raked down, but they missed again. I gained the top of the rise, crashed through some clinging under-growth and hared into the dark corridors formed by the night-shrouded trees.

I could still hear the hoodlums from the car running up the slope. The note of the flying-machine's engine changed to an angry buzz. I glanced upwards and caught a glimpse of it, gaining altitude above the opening in the leafy arches above my head.

The wood was as black as the inside of a shoe-black's gullet, but I kept on running, sometimes blundering into the boles of trees, stumbling over roots and becoming entangled in underbrush.

The helicopter was still flying some-where above the trees. The sound of its spinning vanes seemed to fill the whole atmosphere.

Voices sounded louder against the

whirring from the dark sky, the voices of men who crashed through the under-growth beneath the trees. I gripped the comforting hardness of the Colt's butt and tried to move quickly through the trees and the tangles of underbrush without making a sound. I felt like a hunted animal in that wood, with the exception that an animal would be armed with its natural cunning, whereas I was lost in an alien element.

The voices of the pursuing hoodlums sounded off to one side.

They seemed to have split up into groups.

A raspy baritone shouted: 'Hey, Al, can you see him?'

Al retorted with an unprintable, then: 'Naw. I can't even see my own nose!'

I kept moving stealthily, heading away from the direction of the voices. At least, I wasn't the only one out of his element in this chase. The mugs who were combing the wood were as much sidewalk-pounders as myself.

But the odds were stacked with them.

I did my best to cat-foot among the

trees, trying to suppress even my heavy breathing. I reached the margin of the stand of trees and crouched into some thickly grown bushes.

Deep in the wood, I could hear the searchers crashing through the shrubbery. One of them swore loudly as he fell over something or blundered into a tree.

I hoped he hurt himself.

From where I squatted in the bush, I could see the dark sweep of the highway angling away down below the knoll. Away in the distance were the lights of East Chicago. Men were working the night shift over there and the red and yellow flares of the blast furnaces were reflected as brightly flimmering stabs of light on the surface of Lake Michigan.

A scene not without a certain beauty. If you had time to absorb it.

Which I hadn't, right at that moment.

The Shelmerdine bloodhounds crashed about in the heart of the wood.

The helicopter hovered and whirred somewhere above the trees like an enraged hornet.

And I regained my breath, crouching in the bush.

Along the road, with headlamps flashing, came three cars from the southerly direction. I recognised them. The boys who had tailed me from South Bend.

They braked to a stop down there where the first car was parked. Distance-diminished figures began to issue from the three vehicles. The droning 'copter came creeping over the tree-tops, very low, and passed right over my head. I saw it go whirling down towards the roadway where the figures stood spread-legged, looking up at it.

The flying egg-whisk swooped low over their heads, hanging by its spinning air-screw.

Over the noise of the threshing blades, I heard a wheezy voice shout: 'Lantry's up in the wood somewhere. He's the guy that killed Kornes. Go help find him!'

Shelmerdine's voice.

Some of the visiting firemen from South Bend started up the slope. I could see objects in their hands. The coy moon came out from behind a cloud to put a metallic sheen on the object.

Now, the odds were more than stacked against me.

Shelmerdine's voice was raised again.

'The girl took my car towards East Chicago. Go see if you can locate her!'

The remaining figures climbed into one of the cars and it went speeding off towards the points of light that marked the town.

The small figures were still coming up the knoll. The crashing and raised voices still sounded from the depths of the trees.

I began to angle back along the top of the rise, moving along the margin of the cluster of trees.

I wondered what was happening to Joanne.

Just inside the margin of the high trees, I cat-footed back along the crest of the knoll. Somebody came trudging through crackling undergrowth and I heard a flat nasal voice say: 'He must have given us the slip somehow.'

The voice was too close for comfort and I froze against the bark of a tree. The crashing feet sounded nearer and I saw a pair of vague shadows go walking past, within a yard of the tree against which I was standing.

One shadow said: 'This is the edge of the wood. My guess is he's somewhere in the middle. Let's move back into the centre again.'

'Okay,' agreed the second shadow, stopping his progression. 'First, I'm gonna light a cigarette.'

The other made a noise of disgust.

'Don't be a lunkhead! Ain't you got any sense? That shamus has a gun, suppose he sees the light, he can pick you off in the darkness!'

Quite a woodsman, that guy. Maybe he was a Boy Scout who embarked on a life of crime by running away with the troop funds.

'Yeah,' said the second shadow, as though he had been suddenly enlightened as to all the mysteries of the universe. 'Yeah. Maybe you're right.'

They crashed away into the middle of the trees and I breathed again.

After a while, I started my stealthy progression along the rim of the trees again.

The persistent whirring of the 'copter sounded above the trees once more. Somebody, somewhere in the wood, was shouting: 'Go look over that direction. We'll keep looking over this way.'

Somebody instructing the South Bend hoodlums who had evidently just arrived at the top of the rise.

I kept right on moving along the margin of the trees, saw that the knoll swept down, at its rear side, to a miniature valley. There was a building of some kind down there, it looked like a crumbling old house.

The dawn started stretching itself lazily up in the sky that seemed full of the sound of the helicopter. The clouds began to flush with a gentle rosiness.

Cautiously, I looked upwards. The tune of the helicopter still whirred in the raw morning air, but the machine was out of sight. I decided to make a run for the old building down the slope, broke out of the trees and went haring off, half doubled, trying to merge with the dark ground.

I made good going, too.

Until I was spotted.

There was a yell from up on the tree-crested slope at my back.

A gun barked; a slug whined by my head.

Up above sounded the flying-machine's engine. I looked backwards and up as I ran and saw the helicopter come over the top of the mass of trees, moving against the red-flushed sky like a great, bloated fish swimming out of a clump of seaweed.

I remembered the sub machine-gun that either Shelmerdine or his pilot had raked the knoll with earlier and put on a spurt of speed as the 'copter came bearing down.

The tumbledown old building was perhaps fifty yards away. I had a glimpse of naked rafters outlined against the rose and gold sweep of the sky.

I kept on running.

Another single shot sounded and I felt a hot stab driving into my left leg at the fleshy part of the calf. It burned as if a white hot knife had been thrust into the flesh.

But I kept on running.

13

I made it to the old building.

It had been a house once, a timbered two-storey house that had been burnt out at some time or another. It must have been a long time ago, for the fire-punished timbers were moss-grown now and had a musty, rotten smell about them.

There was enough of the structure left to afford cover from the bullets of the Shelmerdine hoods, though, so I scuttled into what had once been the main door. Inside, there was tumbled, fungus-grown debris. The whole of the upper floor had collapsed inwards and the flame-chamfered rafters slanted brokenly against the dawn.

I pitched myself down behind a pile of musty rubble. I could see out of the doorless main entrance. Dark figures ran down the side of the knoll. The helicopter, with Athelstan Shelmerdine in

247

it, hovered close.

The wound in my leg throbbed in persistent pangs. I could feel a sluggish trickle of wetness inching down into my sock.

I huddled close to the dark pile of rubble, realising that the black chauffeur's outfit I wore would make me almost invisible against it. I cocked the Army Colt, fumbled in my pants pocket and pulled out the spare revolver.

The dark figures were still running down the slope.

High over the stripped rafters, the helicopter came on its spinning vanes. The machine-gun artist up there started his weapon to stuttering, raking the end of the ruin furthermost from where I crouched. He was a long way off target and I realised it was still too dark for me to be seen from the air.

It was no Sunday school picnic, though, lying there while the airborne gunner triggered at random.

Sooner or later, it would be bright enough for them to spot me down there in the old ruin; on the other hand, the remainder of the hoods were coming down the slope in the direction of the old house. Once I fired on them, I would give my position away to Shelmerdine and his pilot.

That couldn't be helped. I wasn't going to just lie there and let those mugs finish me without offering something like a fight.

I took careful aim through the door-space with one of the Colts, triggered it and dropped the leading hood; I fired a second time and saw another dark figure stumble.

The 'copter swooped lower, swinging into a change of course, guided by the position of my barking gun.

On my knees and elbows, holding both revolvers, I scooted out from behind the tumbled debris, the way I had done often enough in war-time combat, and took up a fresh position, lying flat against the wall at the side of the door-space furthest from my first position.

The sub machine-gun in the sky chattered a burst, the bullets slamming close to where I had fired from.

Outside, the hoodlums who had been coming down the slope slackened their speed, but were still advancing cautiously upon the old house. They were temptingly near now, but I had to remember that every shot I fired gave my position away to the gunner in the aircraft. Also, I had to conserve ammunition. One shot fired at the car on the highway, another wild one thrown at the helicopter and two just fired at the running mobsters meant I had only two shots left in one Colt, while the other still had a fully charged cylinder.

I waited until the hoodlums outside drew even nearer to the gutted building. Above the crippled rafters, the flying machine buzzed in a circle. I guessed the machine-gun artist was uncertain as to whether or not that last burst had found me.

Outside, the hoods were almost on what was left of the porch.

But I waited, lying flat and peeking from the doorway.

Then I used the two shots. One of the hoodlums pitched forward like a wooden figure while another scooted backwards, howling on a high pitched note.

Somebody bellowed: 'Look out! He's damned accurate!'

I saw three or four figures running back from the ruins, looking for cover. A spatter of wild shots hit the timbering close to the doorway and the bloated fish in the sky came over towards my position, almost nuzzling the ruined rafters with its rounded nose.

So I crawled out of there on my belly, dumping the useless Colt on the way.

As I expected, the machine-gun started to rattle from the aircraft, the slugs streaking for the spot I had just vacated. I was up against a weed-grown and mould-eaten wall now. The dawn was widening. Soon, I would be as obvious as a bed-bug at the Waldorf.

Outside the doorway, shots were being fired at the burnt-out old structure and the gunner in the sky continued to rake the gloomy interior.

Pretty soon, I'd be a goner if I stayed in there. I was feeling about as comfortable as a long corn in a short shoe.

There was a square of glassless window a little way along the wall against which I crouched, opening to one side of the old building. I edged along towards it, keeping to the musty shadows and moving through the cluster of high-grown weed.

The wound in my leg was throbbing furiously.

Up above, the 'copter nosed around the rafters again, its gun silent for the time being. Some sporadic shots were still being fired at the front of the ruin. The hoods outside must have been shooting at shadows, but they were wasting ammunition and that was all right by me.

I reached the square of window.

I slithered through it, feet first and rump after. There was a patch of weed directly underneath the outside of the window and I landed into it.

I crouched there for a while to catch my breath. The flying egg-whisk was still hovering over the rafters. The dawn was broadening and I didn't like that one bit. In my black chauffeur's coat and cap, I could keep well out of sight in the darkness but, in the first light of the new day, the outfit would make me stand out like a crow on an acacia tree.

Down in the weeds, I squatted, gripping the Colt.

My left sock was soggy, the sticky trickle had reached the sole of my foot. At this side of the house, there was a clutter of wild bushes and more trees beyond them, thick trees a man could hide in, trees that were full of shadow to hide a man in a dark outfit. If only he could get through that tangle of bushes to reach them.

I was thinking about attempting a run through the brush when two sharp-suited figures came around the corner of the ruin. Two of the Shelmerdine hangers-on the big boss had called up to intercept Joanne and myself. They were cheap. They wore loud suits and looked as crummy as a crumb can get; they were lower on the social scale of crookdom than even the black overcoats and soft fedoras.

But they carried guns and were too close to me for me to feel easy.

So I fired.

I hit the leading one in his gun-hand. He dropped his heater with a howl like that of a wounded alley-cat and ran back, clutching his hand. I didn't think he was too badly hurt. He would probably still be able to write out his two-dollar bet — if he was able to write at all, that is.

His pal ran with him, bawling: 'He's round the side of the house!'

Which just about fixed it for me, I figured.

I heard the whirring of Shelmerdine's flying-machine coming over the remains of the gable of the house.

And feet were pounding around to my side of the ruin from the front.

I began to stretch my legs for the undergrowth of bushes separating me from the shelter of the trees. My left leg was aching as if somebody had sneaked up on me and poured a soup-spoonful of hell into my sock.

The sun came to life, big and golden and sudden.

I noticed that as I ran because I figured it was the last time I would ever see it. It was an old friend. I had walked under it for a matter of thirty years and I had grown to like it. Right now, though, it was ratting on me, showing me up as a scuttling black beetle for my enemies to crush.

I made the bushes. They were knee-deep and treacherously tangled.

The hoodlums who came around from the front of the old house opened up. They fired three or four times as I stumbled through the undergrowth. I ducked and kept running. The bullets missed me, but some only got just by without taking pieces of me with them.

I fired a couple of wild shots at the hoodlums, which was a panicky and stupid thing to do because it now left me with only three cartridges in the Army Colt.

The whirring of the hovering aircraft's propeller sounded loud behind me. I went stumbling through the brush. Vaguely, I wondered about Joanne Kilvert and whether those hoods Shelmerdine had sent after her had caught up with her.

I turned and saw the rounded mass of

the forward part of the helicopter very low behind me. The remainder of the mobsters had held off firing, because Athelstan Shelmerdine was standing up in the machine with a Thompson crooked in his arm. He couldn't miss now. They knew it. He knew it and was grinning.

I knew it and, if I grinned. it was a grin of fear.

There was a symbolic touch to the scene. A reversion to what Shelmerdine had been in the old booze-running days. These many years, he had been the big puppet-master, pulling the strings that operated a bunch of cheap hoodlums and made them do his dirty work. He sat in his mansion, read history books, collected paintings, breathed air scented with bees-wax polish and didn't even pack a heater.

Now, he had turned full circle.

The helicopter was a modern touch, but it didn't alter the picture too much. Thirty years ago, it would have been an automobile racing down some obscure Chicago street; but Athelstan Shelmerdine was still what he had been in those days.

A mobster with a rod.

Nothing more.

He was waiting. Standing up and biding his time, holding the Thompson levelled at me. Waiting and grinning while I stumbled through the tangled brush.

The other mobsters were looking on, waiting for the show-down.

I kept staggering and stumbling in the direction of the trees.

I half-turned and fired all my remaining bullets at the hovering machine. They missed, because I was running and panicking, but one starred the tough perspex of the globular body of the machine.

And Shelmerdine grinned. The youthful chauffeur at the controls grinned.

I wondered how many times Shelmerdine had done this before, thirty years ago in the alleys on the territory of whatever Chicago side he ran with.

Giving a man a start. Watching him run down the alley, waiting until he was almost clear, but not quite. Just clear enough to have the hope that he stood half a chance in his heart.

Then gunning him in the back.

I figured Shelmerdine was about to start gunning at any second.

I threw the Colt away. It was empty, useless.

Then I pitched myself down to the roots of the bushes, just as he opened up with the sub machine-gun.

I heard the dry crackle of the weapon and the spatter of the bullets slashing through the greenery. But, I had fooled him. He couldn't see me. I was down in the depths of the shrubbery, crawling quickly off to one side among the soil and roots.

I heard Shelmerdine swear above the rattle of the weapon. He stopped firing and the helicopter came dropping lower. I stopped crawling, so the rustle of the bushes would not betray my position.

Very cautiously, I shoved my head upwards. I could see a small portion of the machine, hovering low enough to be almost touching the tops of the bushes.

I could see the obese form of Shelmerdine, still standing and flourishing the Thompson and the pilot, Cortines, crouching over the controls.

All at once, I remembered the derringer I took from Cortines when I frisked him in the field the day before.

It was still in my pants pocket. I had forgotten it.

I fumbled for it, found it and took aim as the 'copter nosed a little nearer my position.

When I fired, I fired at Cortines.

The perspex of the rounded windshield shattered. I couldn't miss at that range. Cortines stiffened back in his seat, then he slumped over the controls.

I started crawling for a new position as Shelmerdine whirled about.

I kept crawling until I heard a shrill yell, accentuated by the fact that the whirring of the 'copter's blades had ceased. I shoved my head up far enough to see the machine plummeting down into the brush and in a strangely slowed-down fashion. I saw Shelmerdine falling out of the craft, like a man being pitched from a boat.

Cortines must have fallen across something that cut the engine.

The helicopter landed in the shrubbery with a terrific crash. It bounced on its skids and heeled over on to its side.

A voice was screaming horribly and hoarsely from the direction of the machine and I got up into a low crouch and went haring towards it. I realised dimly that Shelmerdine had thrown the Thompson outwards as he fell and I wanted it.

I was aware of the remaining hoods running towards the overturned machine.

The hoarse voice was yelling. No words, just yelling and yelling.

I found the sub machine-gun lying close to the 'copter.

The yelling was coming from Shelmerdine. He was pinned under the weight of the overturned machine. Only the upper third of his body was visible and he was yelling and yelling.

I didn't feel the least bit sorry for him this time.

With the sub machine-gun in my hand, I waited until the hoods got a little nearer. Then I gave them a short burst.

It was enough. Two dropped and the

rest went running back.

Shelmerdine was still yelling.

If he'd been an injured dog, I would have shot him to put him out of pain.

But he wasn't anything half so worthy as a dog in my book.

I stood there, my leg throbbing madly. I was prepared to stand there and give the mobsters the remainder of the magazine if anyone showed any fight.

Maybe I was just a little crazy at that moment.

A voice called: 'Hold it, Lantry! Hold it!'

I saw figures coming forward from the direction of the tree-crested hill, figures in civilian suits, figures in police uniforms and a slim feminine one in a flowered summer dress.

I didn't believe it.

The mobsters were giving themselves up. There wasn't an ounce of fight left in them. I guess every one of them was wishing he'd stayed in the pool halls of Gary Bend right then. The cops had their bracelets out in nothing flat.

Shelmerdine's screeching died in a

gurgling squawk.

It was Walt Toland who came forward and dropped a hand on my shoulder.

'Better late than never, chief,' he grinned.

'It was damn near never,' I said. 'How did you manage to pick up the state police on the way? I didn't think there were any cops left in the world.'

'They came just natural. When we arrived at the highway back there, they were standing around wondering why so many cars were parked across the roadway and pondering on the near-by shooting.'

A hefty figure with a crew-cut and an arm in a sling came out of the cluster of cops, World Wide Investigations men and mobsters.

'Hi, Lantry!'

'Jack Kay! What brought you in on this?'

'When your boys came down from Chicago the other day, they stopped by at our place for a brief check-up on what had happened. I joined them for this little run around Indiana. It was like the old days in France, but not quite so much shooting,' he grinned. 'Now let's get back home for a bite to eat. Beth will give me hell for staying away this long.'

'I'll come back to South Bend,' I told him, 'but it'll be to see the cops about that stiff I planted on your lawn.'

'Strikes me you'll be commended for that, Mike, not blamed. The cops came nosing around our place after you lit out and intimated that Speedy Kornes was no loss to anybody. You shot in defence of a third party, which makes it pretty clear for you and the radio calls for your arrest were strictly routine because you took it on the lam after the shooting.'

Joanne Kilvert was standing a little coyly at one side.

'So you made it,' I commented.

She nodded.

'And you didn't get caught by the nasty ruffians Athelstan sent after you?'

She shook her head.

'No. I reached a service station in East Chicago, 'phoned Chicago as you told me, then I decided to make a temporary trade with the owner. I gave him that conspicuous big car for a beaten up old coupe. He thought I was mad, of course, but I drove back here, just in time to meet the police and tell them what was happening. Your investigators arrived a short time later.'

I forced a grin.

'Smart kid. So you passed Shelmerdine's lugs somewhere on the way, and the change of cars fooled them. Any time you want a job as a lady shamus, come to World Wide. I think you're okay, too.'

The mobsters were handcuffed and a senior policeman came forward, with a friendly smile which is unusual when a public cop faces a private one.

'Seems you've been instrumental in busting up a big combine, Mr. Lantry,' he praised.

My injured leg remembered to start aching again and I got slightly irritable.

'Stick around, O'Callaghan,' I said. 'Wait until World Wide puts certain papers into the hands of the Crime Commission. You're in for some fun. You'll see a lot of people in high places suddenly falling into low ones. Meanwhile, you'll find more

Shelmerdine hoods in the custody of the Sheriff at Stokestown.'

Jack Kay fished in his hip pocket and produced a whisky flask. He fisted it into my hand. You can't beat a sensible married and settled-down man for applying good judgement at the right time.

'Take a swig, Mike, you look peaked.'

It tasted good.

'Boy!' I breathed, gratefully. 'I intend to have three or four more stiff drinks right after I have a slug taken from my leg and square myself with the South Bend police about that shooting match.'

'Then what?' asked Jack Kay.

'Then a meal and a long, long sleep.'

'And then?' asked the elfin-featured Joanne.

I looked at the cute face that could get to grow on one.

'After the schemozzle you got me into, girlie, another vacation — what else?'

We do hope that you have enjoyed reading this large print book.

Did you know that all of our titles are available for purchase?

We publish a wide range of high quality large print books including:
Romances, Mysteries, Classics
General Fiction
Non Fiction and Westerns

Special interest titles available in large print are:
The Little Oxford Dictionary
Music Book, Song Book
Hymn Book, Service Book

Also available from us courtesy of Oxford University Press:
Young Readers' Dictionary
(large print edition)
Young Readers' Thesaurus
(large print edition)

For further information or a free brochure, please contact us at:
Ulverscroft Large Print Books Ltd.,
The Green, Bradgate Road, Anstey,
Leicester, LE7 7FU, England.
Tel: (00 44) **0116 236 4325**
Fax: (00 44) **0116 234 0205**